Book Fair 1999

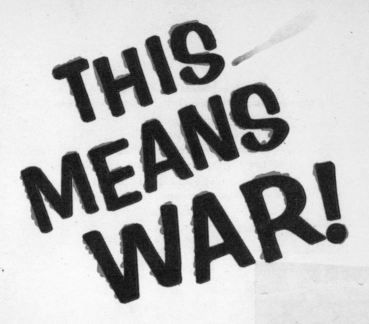

THIS MEANS WAR!

Bev Spencer

Cover by
Tony Meers

Scholastic Canada Ltd.

Scholastic Canada Ltd.
123 Newkirk Road, Richmond Hill, Ontario, Canada L4C 3G5
Scholastic Inc.
555 Broadway, New York, NY 10012, USA
Scholastic Australia Pty Limited
PO Box 579, Gosford, NSW 2250, Australia
Scholastic New Zealand Limited
Private Bag 94407, Greenmount, Auckland, New Zealand
Scholastic Ltd.
Villiers House, Clarendon Avenue, Leamington Spa,
Warwickshire CV32 5PR, UK

Canadian Cataloguing in Publication Data
Spencer, Bev.
This means war!
ISBN 0-590-12440-4
I. Title.
PS8587.P32M42 1998   jC813'.54   C97-931862-9
PZ7.S63Me 1998

5 4 3 2 1   Printed and Bound in Canada   8 9 /9 0 1 2 /0

With affectionate thanks to Joyce

PRIVATE!! DO NOT READ!!!

THIS MEANS YOU, ROGER!!!

Turn this page and I'll tell Mom what happened to her best blouse. And if you think I don't know, let me say one word — KITE!

Chapter 1

After school today I found Roger hiding in Old Man Trumpkin's bushes, spying on Mr. Wooley through a rolled-up "telescope." He had his shoulders hunched against the cool November wind and the telescope glued to his eye. Roger had tried leaning out of our third-floor apartment windows to peer into Mr. Wooley's windows on the second floor, but he hadn't been able to see much from there. From Mr. T's bushes he could see all of the big old three-storey house where we lived.

"Get out of there, Roger," I said, resisting the urge to throttle him on the spot. World Famous Reporters aren't supposed to throttle people. "Do you want Mr. Trumpkin to yell at Mom?"

"*Shhh!* No one can see me here."

"Half the planet can see you. And you're smashing the bushes to pieces! Mom told you never to go into Mr. Trumpkin's bushes again." Roger has a talent for smashing things.

"Shut up. I almost saw Mr. Wooley this time."

"If you want to see Mr. Wooley why don't you just knock on his apartment door?"

"Because I've got to see him when he doesn't *know* I'm seeing him. If I knocked on his door he'd have time to hide his secret." Roger shook his head, pitying me. "Everyone knows that!"

"Hide what secret, Roger?"

"If I knew his secret, would I be hiding here? Get down, Laney. He might see us."

"Roger! You've got to stop reading *True Tales of the Bizarre*. The world is not full of freaky mysteries."

"Yes it is. Remember the guy in the news with forty-two cats? The news you're always making us watch?"

"How can I expect to change the world if I don't know what's going on? Watching the news is good for you."

"Watching the news is boring, except for the cat story. That guy was weird! Only, Mr. Wooley doesn't have forty-two cats. He has something even creepier, and he can't let anyone see inside his apartment or they'll take him away in a straight jacket. That's why he's a reeckfloose."

"That's *recluse,* Roger — a person who never goes out."

"But what's he hiding?" Roger narrowed his eyes. "Maybe it's something from outer space."

"*You're* the one from outer space. Try living on the planet Earth. Now get out of there!"

"In a second. So, what if Mr. Wooley had a *million* cats, only he was experimenting on them with a germ from outer space. And they all died of a nasty disease and now he has them pickled in jars, all the tails in one room, all the heads in another, all the — "

"Roger, you're gross!"

"Thank you." He grinned.

"Hey, what did you use to make that telescope? You creep, that's my science project! Give it back."

I grabbed hold of my rolled-up project and pulled. Roger pulled back.

"It was the only paper the right size!" he said. "I didn't get it dirty or nothin'. Let go."

"*You* let go!"

Roger gave up pulling and shoved me. The two of us crashed down in the bushes.

"Hooligans! Barbarians!" Mr. Trumpkin shouted, running out of his house. He grabbed hold of us by the ears and dragged us out of his bushes.

Roger howled, "My ear! You're killing my ear."

I was too humiliated to speak.

"Look what you've done to my golden Pfitzer juniper. You ruffians!"

Roger turned to Old Man T with wide-eyed innocence. "I *told* my sister not to go in your bushes. But she never listens to me. Do you, Laney?"

Old Man Trumpkin let go of Roger and scowled at me. "So it was you!" he said.

"But Mr. Trumpkin — "

"Don't interrupt," he yelled.

While Mr T's attention was on me, Roger sprinted for home. For at least twenty minutes Old Man T lectured me about respecting other people's property. He wouldn't believe I was innocent. "Shame on you, trying to blame your sweet young brother. And another thing . . . "

I had to rake up all the broken branches, and help trim Mr. Trumpkin's lawn. "What's right is right," he said. *Hah!*

As I left I grabbed my project from the rubble. It was crushed and covered with dirt. I tried out several headlines in my head. My favourite was GIRL MAILS BROTHER TO ANTARCTICA. JURY FINDS HER NOT GUILTY ON ACCOUNT OF THE BROTHER BEING TOTALLY IRRITATING!

I found Roger smirking on our front porch. "You rotten stinking liar!" I said.

"It's not nice to call your sweet little brother names!" He jumped over the railing as I got close. "We're not supposed to fight. Mom said so. Remember, Laney?"

I gritted my teeth. "I'm going to have to do this whole project again, you rat! Do you know how long it took me to do this graph?"

"It's your fault," Roger said righteously. "I only dropped the telescope because you grabbed it."

"Stay out of Mr. Trumpkin's bushes!"

"But it's the only place to hide. How else am I going to find out about Mr. Wooley?" Roger asked. Then he leered. "Maybe *he's* from outer space, and he's so ugly people scream when they see him. Maybe that's why he never goes anywhere."

"Maybe he doesn't want to get run over by Roger Hadley, the Human Wrecking Ball!"

"That's not fair," Roger whined. "We only moved in five months ago. Mr. Wooley stopped going out long before that — as long as Miss Applebaum's been living below him. She told me."

"Miss Applebaum likes to talk. Maybe Mr. Wooley doesn't."

"Well, if he's from outer space he might not be able to talk. He might not even have a face, just two holes in a green blob on top of his neck. He can only grunt."

"How would he order his groceries, then?" We had all seen the delivery man put bags of groceries in the old-fashioned milk box built into the wall by Mr. Wooley's apartment door.

"He has a code," Roger said. "One grunt for canned spaghetti. Two for milk — "

"Roger . . . "

"All right," Roger said. "But you'll be sorry when I find out the truth and I don't tell you. By the way, you're a mess."

"What?" I looked down at myself. Bits of muddy bush were stuck to me in three places. My best jeans were torn at the knee. I made a grab for Roger. He slipped by me. "You are such a *disease*, Roger!" I shouted.

LANEY'S LAW NUMBER 31:
Younger brothers are illegal. If they exist they should sent to Antarctica.

Life was a lot better when I could pin Roger's arms with one hand and sit on him until he apologized. Everyone knows this is the sacred right of an older sister.

In the big doorway to the house Roger ran into our landlord, Mr. Dutton, who was coming out. Mr. Dutton's briefcase went flying.

"Watch out, boy! Don't you know how to use a door? Or are you going to break that too?" Dutton growled. He was about two metres tall. His brown hair was parted at the side and seemed to be glued down.

"That's not fair," Roger said. "I hardly broke nothin'."

He had broken the mailbox, the doorbell, a window and two kitchen cupboards, so far, but who's counting? Maybe Mr. Dutton was. He had made a big fuss about making Mom pay for the repairs.

"Why don't you look where you're going?" Dutton snarled, scooping up his briefcase and brushing it off.

"Yeah?" Roger snapped. "Well why don't you look where *you're* going?"

Behind Mr. Dutton, Miss Applebaum appeared, shaking her fist at him. Her face was as red as her hair. Her pointed nose was even redder. A full-sleeved red and white blouse billowed out around her. She looked a lot like a fire truck going at full speed.

"How could you carry through with this outrage? You have ignored my letters of appeal. Very well! I will take you to court, sir!" she cried. "I will prosecute you with the greatest vigour — "

"It won't do you any good," Dutton said, scowling. "I am completely within my legal rights. This is a business matter; don't make it into a soap opera. You have one month left to vacate the premises." He looked down on us as if we were slimy insects. "You *all* have to vacate the premises."

"Vacate?" Roger repeated.

Dutton looked at him. "Children," he sneered. He crossed the porch and was down the stairs to the sidewalk before I could react.

LANEY'S LAW NUMBER 32:
The trouble with tall people is they always look down on you.

"We're going on vacation?" Roger asked.

"It's not a vacation," I said.

Mr. Dutton reached his car, started it noisily and drove off.

"I do *not* like *that man*," Miss Applebaum said, her eyes flashing.

"Who?" Roger looked at her with interest. "Mr. Wooley?"

"No. Mr. Dutton. He and his legal rights! A travesty of justice! What good does it do to talk about these things, you may say. Talk is cheap. You're right. But you haven't heard the last of this matter! Forgive my rudeness, children, but one has a great deal to do." Miss Applebaum disappeared through her first-floor apartment door like a small tornado.

Roger frowned. "It has to be a vacation," he said. "I heard him say 'vacate.'"

"Vacate means move out, Roger," I said.

"What?" Roger gulped. *"Mo-om!"*

Roger went up the stairs like a missile, yelling louder than usual. He didn't even stop to snoop in Mr. Wooley's milk box on the second floor, the way he did a dozen times every day. He was through the door to our third-floor apartment in record time.

Chapter 2

"Mr. Dutton says we have to vacate, Mom. Tell me he's lying!"

"He's not lying, Roger," Mom said, with a look of tired patience. "Sit down. Elaine. Emma, you too. I want to talk to all of you at once."

LANEY'S LAW NUMBER 33:
When Mom calls me Elaine, this is a very bad sign.

There were glasses of milk and Oreos waiting for us on the chipped wooden kitchen table. Oreos are expensive. Mom only buys them when she has bad news to tell us. Emma pushed her blond curls out of her eyes and filled her hands with Oreos. She tried to stuff two into her mouth at once. When that didn't work she took one apart and started licking the filling, and her fingers, and her nose (at least trying).

LANEY'S LAW NUMBER 34:
Little kids are gross, especially little sisters.

I sat down. Roger banged his chair.

"Roger, please," Mom said.

He sat.

"Brace yourselves, children," Mom said. "We're going to have to move again."

"But, we've only been here five months!" Roger said. "I haven't even seen Mr. Wooley yet. We can't move now." Roger's voice was loud enough to break eardrums. I nudged him under the table.

"Ow!" he cried, scowling at me.

Emma got up and yelled, "I won't move! I won't move!" at the top of her lungs.

"Emma," Mom said.

Emma bolted to the counter, opened a cupboard and climbed onto the countertop, where she sat glaring at us.

"Emma, come and sit at the table with the rest of us."

"Won't come. Won't!"

"All right, you can listen from there."

"What happened, Mom?" I asked. "I thought you signed a one-year lease."

"So did I." There was a dejected look on Mom's face.

She spread out a letter on the table. "Mr. Dutton just delivered the second notice. We're being evicted."

"What's edicted?" Roger shouted.

"*Evicted*," I said. "It means thrown out."

"Thrown out?" Roger sputtered. "What for? I haven't done anything wrong. The mailbox was already cracked. It's not my fault."

"No one is saying it's your fault, Roger. We don't have to do anything wrong to be evicted. I got the first notice awhile ago, but I didn't want to worry you. Mr. Dutton spoke of us living here for years, but now he wants to turn the apartments into condominiums and sell them. Legally, he's allowed to do that. All the tenants will have to leave."

"Wait a minute," I said. "There must be a law — "

Mom shook her head. "I wish you were right. I've talked to a lot of people, including City Hall. I had an appointment with a tenant's association last night. Until then I thought we could fight this, but there's nothing we can do. Now we have one month left to find another place to live."

"But that means we'll have to move just before Christmas," Roger yelped.

"Moving isn't fun, but it isn't the end of the world either. We *will* survive this," Mom said. "We'll be fine!" She looked over at Emma.

"Where will we go?" I asked.

"If we go to Great Aunt Florence's again I'll — I'll — " Roger was actually speechless for a moment. "She fined me my whole allowance for four months!"

"You made a banner out of her best linen table-cloth," Mom said.

"There was nothing else the right size. It was a dumb tablecloth anyway."

I nudged him again, harder. "What?" he asked. "What did I say wrong?"

"Florence can't have us," Mom went on. "She's going to Europe."

"We could stay there without her," Roger suggested.

Mom sighed. "Florence seems to think her house would not be safe with us in it. None of your great-aunts will have us back — at least not all of us at once. They have vivid memories of our last visits." She looked at Roger.

"Why do I get blamed for everything?" he asked.

"I will do my best to find us a new place to live this month, but if I can't . . . " Mom's determined look wavered. "Then Aunt Gladys — "

"Aunt Gladys tried to have me *arrested*," Roger yelped. "She *hates* me."

"It was wrong of you to loan her African death masks to your friends for Halloween."

"They were just hanging on the wall, doing nothin'."

"I promised Gladys there would be no trouble like that again." Mom's look was stern. "Let me finish, Roger. Aunt Gladys will take you, Elaine. Aunt Joyce will take Emma and me, and Aunt Sybil will let Roger stay with her until we find a place."

"Won't go! Won't," Emma said.

Roger slid down in his seat until his nose touched the table. "Aunt Sybil won't let me watch UFO stories."

"Aunt Sybil has the right to say what you watch on her TV," Mom said.

"Miss Applebaum is taking Dutton to court," I said. "Why can't we do that?"

"Because we can't afford a lawyer," Mom said, "and long legal battles are actually worse than moving."

Roger started banging his foot against the table leg.

"Stop that, Roger. I'm going to start apartment hunting tonight." There were lines around Mom's eyes. I had never noticed them before.

"You can do it, can't you?" Roger asked. "I mean you can find another apartment close by, so I can keep investigating Mr. Wooley."

Mom shook her head. "I'm afraid not. You know how hard it was to find this place. This is the last old house with apartments for rent in this neighbourhood. We can't afford the rents in the highrises around here."

"TENANTS EVICTED SO LANDLORD CAN GET RICH," I said. "We can't let him do this to us, Mom!"

"We can't stop him, Laney." Mom passed a thin hand over her forehead, pushing wispy brown curls out of her face. She glanced at her watch. "I've made some appointments on the east side."

"The east side?" Roger spit out. "That's eons away! We might as well move to the North Pole."

"It's not as bad as that," Mom said. "We'll have to start over, but we've done that before. We'll be fine."

"Not me! I'll never be fine again." Roger stormed from the kitchen.

Mom sighed. I left her talking quietly to Emma. When I got to the living room Roger glared at me.

"What's that for?" I asked, glaring back.

"For poking me under the table. I wasn't doing anything wrong!"

"You were yelling at Mom. It's not her fault we have to move. I don't see why you care about moving, anyway."

"You don't see anything. Do you know how often a real mystery comes along? Once in a zillion years! Mr. Wooley is a real live mystery. He hasn't left his apartment *once* in over fifteen years. That's how ginormous his secret is."

I frowned. "He has to leave his apartment to put his garbage out."

"No he doesn't. He sends it down the dumbwaiter and Mr. Trumpkin puts it out."

"Oh. Well, that's not such a big deal. Maybe he has trouble walking or something."

Roger shook his head. "I stayed in the hall outside his door for hours last week and I *heard* him walking. Look at this." Roger held up a *True Tales of the Bizarre* comic for me to see. "They print your name and your picture when they put your mystery in the comic. This kid's cow had a calf with two heads!" Roger gave the picture of the calf an admiring look. "I wish we had cows! I've been waiting for a mystery like Mr. Wooley my whole life! Forever! Everyone could read about how I solved the bizarre mystery of the hidden man! I'd be famous! I'd win the contest for the best mystery of the year. And with the cash prize I'd buy *all* the *True Tales* comics — hundreds of them. Zillions of bizarre stories!"

"You don't really believe those stupid stories, do you?"

"Of course I do. They're true, every one of them."

I flipped through the comic. "But this one's about a UFO!"

"Just because it's not on the boring news doesn't mean it isn't true," Roger snapped. "I knew you wouldn't understand. Now I'll never know about Mr. Wooley, and I'll never get my name in *True Tales*, and I'll never win the money, because we have to move. And you don't even care!" Roger poked me.

"Watch who you're poking!" I said. I pushed his hand away. It would feel so good to sit on him, but I couldn't do that anymore. "At least the news is true!" I made the worst face at him that I could, wrinkling my nose. He pulled his mouth to the side with his finger and stuck his tongue out over his chin. "You're such a creep, Roger! Leave me alone."

Emma came in just as I was curling up in my favourite chair, at a safe distance from Roger, watching the news.

"You're sitting on Winson!" Emma yelled as I sat down.

"Who?"

"Winson Churchall. She's turning purple. Get off her!" Emma was wailing now.

"You had to watch that program on TV last night," Roger said to me. "You had to give The Kid ideas."

"Winston Churchill was the Prime Minister of Britain a long time ago, Emma," I said carefully. *"He's* dead now."

"No she isn't. You can tell by looking at her," Emma said. "Now get *off* her!"

I gritted my teeth. "I'm sitting on a chair, Emma, not a Prime Minister. Chairs aren't alive. They're meant for sitting on."

"Mo-om!" Roger yelled. "Emma's doing it again."

Mom came in from the kitchen wiping her hands. "What?"

"The imaginary friend thing."

"I don't mage nary anything!" Emma said. "Laney's sitting on Winson! She's killing her!"

Mom gave us a determined smile. "Emma seems to have a new friend, Laney. I'm sure you didn't notice you were sitting on her."

We should never let Emma watch television.

"You're mashing Winson!" Emma cried. "She's dying!"

"Aren't any of your friends visible, Emma?" I asked — big mistake, because all her visible friends, and ours, had been left behind two moves and three visits ago. Her face fell. I got up and moved to a hard chair.

"Tell Winson you're sorry," Emma said, pouting.

"I'm not telling a chair I'm sorry!"

"Please, Elaine," Mom said. "Remember what the t-e-a-c-h-e-r advised last time."

"I'm sorry, Winston," I said.

"Emma," Mom said. "We need to have another talk."

Emma stuffed half a cookie into her mouth. "You can moof if you wan' to. I'm sfaying here wif Winfon!" she declared. Pieces of half-chewed Oreo flew in all directions. Emma swallowed. Then she stood on the couch and yelled at the top of her lungs. "We're not moving! *Ever!*"

I gave up trying to watch the news.

LANEY'S LAW NUMBER 35:
Twelve-year-olds should be able to stand on the couch and yell at the top of their lungs like five-year-olds do.

For a long time after that I sat in my room re-reading the note my teacher had written me:

Dear Elaine,
I'm pleased to say you have been chosen to be editor of our school newspaper. I know you'll do a good job. Congratulations!

Mr. Wyman

Then I carefully put it back on my bulletin board. Mary Jean McClintock edited the school newspaper every single year in our old school, before we moved out of our house. I hadn't been at any school since then long enough to get the job, until now.

So much for that!

Roger snuck up behind me later that night. I was working at the kitchen table.

"So what's the World Famous Reporter doing?"

The day Roger stole my "What I want to be" essay from my room and read it, I should have throttled him on the spot and gotten it over with. "I'm trying to redo my science project, Roger," I said. "Do you remember the one? It got squashed in the mud. The teacher said he'd deduct three marks for every day a project is late. Thanks to you, I might flunk science! Leave me alone."

"Some reporter!" Roger snorted.

"What?"

"Here's Dutton, practically stealing our home from under us, and what are you doing? Working on a stupid science project!"

"What do you expect me to do?"

"Change the world, like you always say you're going to. Fix Dutton so he can't do this to us."

"You mean fix him so *you* can win the contest. You're such a child, Roger! I can't *fix* an adult."

"Oh, yeah?" Roger sputtered. "Well I'd rather be a child than what you are. You're a fake!"

"A fake?" I stood up so quickly I knocked my graph aside. My project slid over the table into a bottle of white-out. The bottle tipped and emptied all over the new graph. "Roger, you ruined my new graph! I'm going to throttle you," I shouted.

"No you won't," Roger said, dodging out of reach. "*You* knocked the bottle over."

I managed to scoop some of the white-out back into the bottle, but the graph was ruined. "I'm going to my room now, Roger," I said between clenched teeth. "If you speak to me again tonight you'll be sorry!"

That night I had trouble getting to sleep. Around me I smelled old wood and lemon wax and meat loaf and fresh brownies and newspapers and just the right amount of dust — the smells of home.

Dad's funeral had smelled of flowers, five years ago. I don't remember Dad much anymore. But lying in bed I remembered the house we'd had before Mom lost her job. It was a lot like this place — worn around the edges, rumpled in the right places. I remembered the "visits" — with each aunt, in their starched homes, smelling of Javex and Lysol. We were bound to end up there, probably for months. Well, not exactly "we." No more Human Wrecking Ball, I thought, the champion Destroyer of Graphs, with the overworked imagination. No more Weird Emma and her imaginary friends. I should be feeling overjoyed. So why wasn't I?

I got up to get a drink of water. Someone was in the bathroom, and there were strange sounds coming through the door. "Mom?" I called. "Are you okay?"

"Yes, Elaine. Fine," she called.

The toilet flushed. It flushed twice more before Mom came out.

"I saw some very good prospects tonight," Mom said. "We'll get a place even better than this one."

"Sure, Mom." I put my arm around her and we hugged. "Mom, do you sometimes wish Dad was still around?" I asked.

Her arms tightened around me. "All the time."

"I can't remember much about him."

"That's okay," Mom said, standing with her arm around me. "I can remember for you. All of us miss him, you know, even your brother. We may not think about how much we miss him, but we do just the same. It's hard not having a father. I know that's one of the reasons Roger and Emma behave the way they do." She smoothed my hair. "But they'll get over it eventually. These things just take a lot of time." She gave me another hug. "We lost someone very special when we lost your father."

I nodded. Neither of us said anything else for awhile.

"Your father didn't want to get sick, you know," Mom finally said. "He didn't want to leave us."

"I know, Mom."

"And nothing that happened since is anyone's fault."

"I know."

"Good. Remember that. And remember, we're going to be fine. Now go to sleep. There's nothing to worry about."

"Okay, Mom. 'Night."

LANEY'S LAW NUMBER 36:
Moms are terrible liars.

20

How long could I take Aunt Gladys, I wondered. She plays bridge four nights a week. There is no TV allowed on bridge nights, and no news shows allowed ever. Aunt Gladys thinks the news is a bad influence on young people. ("The news story I saw last week! Well, I won't tell you.") Newspapers aren't allowed in her house because they "turn your hands black and clutter up the house." She also thinks every bite of food should be chewed forty times before swallowing. ("The number of digestive problems which are caused by poor chewing! Well, I won't tell you.") I got tired of hearing about the things she wouldn't tell us. She also talked about us as if we were dogs. I overheard her telling Mom we weren't quite housebroken. Aunt Gladys is, Mom says, a woman of strong opinions.

Poor Emma, I thought. Poor Roger. Someone should really do something.

I thought of more headlines. LANDLORD THROWS DEFENCELESS CHILDREN INTO STREET! Yes — it sounded better every time I tried it out in my head.

I got up and wrote it down before I forgot it. (In my notebook, as usual. When I'm a world famous reporter I'll get to write on a computer, because I'll be rich enough to *spit* money!)

Chapter 3

Told Mr. Wyman I couldn't edit the school newspaper. I knew I'd be gone before the first edition came out after Christmas. I couldn't bring myself to tell him that part.

When I got home from school that afternoon the curtains at one of the second-floor windows twitched as I walked up to the porch. The curtains did that a lot when we were outside playing. That didn't mean Mr. Wooley was weird. Maybe he was just nosey, like Roger.

Caught Roger standing outside Mr. Wooley's apartment with a glass pressed against the door, and his ear pressed against the glass. "Roger, you know what Mom said about snooping. Get away from Mr. Wooley's door."

"Shhh!" he whispered. "I can hear voices. He's got somebody in there with him."

"So he's got a visitor. There's nothing wrong with that."

"Yes there is. Miss Applebaum says he never has visitors. He's an arch-criminal, see, and he kidnapped someone a zillion years ago and he's kept him in a birdcage ever since!"

"A birdcage?"

"Don't talk so loud. A really big birdcage."

"Roger, if he had kidnapped someone, we would hear the person calling for help. Have you ever heard yelling from the second floor?"

Roger veered away as I made a grab for the glass. "Okay, so Mr. Wooley's got two heads, and they argue with each other. Wow — a man with two heads! That would win the contest for sure! That's why he never goes out. People would faint if they saw him."

"Roger!"

"But I heard talking. I did!"

I got hold of the glass. Roger tried to snatch it back. The glass hit the floor and broke.

"Laney! You broke Mom's favourite glass," Roger shouted, and tore up the stairs.

I heard shuffling from inside Mr. Wooley's apartment. There are coloured shadows on the second floor landing, from dark panes of stained glass in the windows. For a second I thought they moved. I ducked up the stairs to get the broom and dustpan, going fast only because of Roger. Really.

It took me fifteen minutes to sweep up all the slivers of glass, and all that time I tried not to turn my back on Mr. Wooley's door. This is ridiculous! I told myself. But I didn't feel comfortable until I was back up in our own apartment.

My favourite time of day is when I watch the news on television, and I pretend I'm sitting in front of the camera, telling the world important things. I am practising a look of serious intelligence. I didn't enjoy it today, though.

"That's Winson's cookie," Emma said.

I ground my teeth together and gave her my cookie. She fed it to the air, making munching sounds, nibbled it, then made a face.

"Yuck! There's a peanut in this cookie. Winson doesn't like peanuts."

She handed it back to me. It was wet.

"Thanks a lot!" I said. Roger laughed.

"Once Winston starts a cookie, she has to finish it," Mom said.

"Oh," Emma said. She took the cookie back, crumbled it up and put it in her pocket. "All finished!"

Mom sighed.

"Did you find us a new house yet?" Roger asked, scowling.

"No. I did look at some two-bedroom apartments but they were too small for us."

"Did you say *two*-bedroom?" I asked.

"Yes." Mom nodded. "We can't afford anything bigger. This apartment is unusually large, as I told you."

"Where will we all sleep?" Roger squawked.

"I'll sleep on the sofa bed, Elaine and Emma will have to share, and — "

"What?" I said. "I need to have my own room. Why can't Roger share with Emma?"

"Because boys and girls don't share rooms. Roger will have a separate room."

"Hah, hah!" Roger said. "You get to live with Winston and the nutbar!"

"Roger, don't call your sister names."

Emma frowned. "Did he call me a nut? Is that a good thing or a bad thing?"

"A good thing," Mom said.

"Oh. Okay . . . But Winson and I aren't moving."

"We talked about this, Emma," Mom said. "Don't you remember?"

"Won't move," Emma said loudly. She climbed up onto the back of the big stuffed chair and Mom had to make her get down.

"You'd think you were a monkey instead of a little girl, Emma, with all this climbing!" Mom shook her head and gave Emma a hug. "Everything's going to be okay, you'll see. I'm going to make dinner now."

I turned up the news.

"Do you like Winson's dress, Laney?" Emma said.

"Sure," I said.

"You're not even looking at it. Laney. *Laney!*"

"Not now, Emma. I'm doing important things."

"What's important about the news?"

"News changes the world. *That's* how important it is."

"But Winson has a new dress and you're hurting her feelings. If you don't look at her she's going to cry."

I looked. "It's a nice dress."

Em grinned. "What colour is it?"

"I said it's nice. What difference does the colour make?"

"What colour *is it?*"

"Blue?"

"Wrong."

"Red?"

"Wrong."

"Yellow?"

"Wrong."

"Green?"

"Wrong."

Emma frowned. "I think maybe you need new glasses. Guess again."

"Emma!"

"You have to be nice to Winson and me. Mama said so. Guess again. Come on. Guess again. Guess again. Guess again. Guess — "

"Pink?"

"Wrong."

"Orange?"

"Wrong."

"White?"

"Wrong! I don't know what's wrong with you, Laney."

I stood up. "I'm going to my room. Don't follow me. I want to be alone. I don't *care* what colour Winston's dress is."

BUDDING REPORTER DRIVEN MAD BY WEIRD SISTER — maybe I could work that into my article.

Emma ran after me. "It's purple! Anyone can see Winson's dress is purple! You'd better get new glasses 'cause you can't see *anything!*"

"Emma, this is *my* room. Keep out!"

"After we move your room will be my room too!"

I slammed the door.

LANEY'S LAW NUMBER 37:
Little sisters should be sent to the same place as little brothers, only sooner.

Later Roger was slumped on the couch, his nose in a copy of *True Tales of the Bizarre*. On the cover was a snake swallowing a bus. "He never opens his curtains," Roger muttered. "Why can't he get his groceries delivered to the door so I can watch? I'll never figure him out in time."

"Roger, how is this move going to affect you?" I asked.

"I already told you, and I'm sorry I did." Roger

looked up. "Why are you asking?"

"No reason," I said quickly. "Have you seen Emma?"

"Not for awhile. What do you want her for?"

"Nothing." I scribbled some words in my notebook.

"Hey! What are you up to?" Roger asked.

"None of your business."

He lunged for the notebook. I ducked out of the way. He put his elbows in my face. The notebook slid out of my hands.

Roger was on it like a rat on cheese. "You're writing a thing for the newspaper, aren't you?"

"No!" I tried to grab the notebook back, but he ducked behind the couch.

"Yes you are. It's right here. HELPLESS CHILDREN THROWN OUT BY HEARTLESS LANDLORD. Tell me."

"Not likely!" I scrambled over the couch.

Roger dodged behind the big chair. "Tell me or I'm telling Mom about it."

"You tell her and you'll be limping for years!"

Mom had gone out apartment hunting again. I wanted to get the article finished before she got back.

"You don't scare me," Roger said. "You're writing about Dutton and what he's doing to us, aren't you? Maybe you're not a fake. You might as well tell me because I know now anyway. And unless you want Mom to know — "

"I hate you, Roger!"

He grinned. "I know."

"All right. At first I was going to put the article in the school newspaper, but this is bigger than that. I'm going to get it in the *Daily News*."

"The big city newspaper? Really?" Roger looked impressed. "How?" He handed back my notebook.

"They'll have to print it when they read it."

Roger's eyes narrowed. "How will that help?"

"People will read about how horrible Dutton is, and they won't want to buy the condominiums. When he can't sell them, we'll get to stay here."

Roger frowned. "What if they want to buy them anyway, and they don't care how horrible Dutton is?"

"They'll care."

"Why?"

I glowered at him. "You haven't even taken journalism in school yet. You don't know about the power of the press. Newspaper articles change the world. Mr. Wyman says so."

"What if he's wrong?"

"Teachers are never wrong. Don't you know anything? Okay, now I have to interview you for quotes about how you feel about Dutton evicting us."

"I don't want to be interviewed."

"Roger! I have to interview everyone. That way I write a balanced article. That's what a good reporter does."

"Everyone? Even Mr. Wooley?"

"Yes."

Roger got a cunning look. "Okay, you can interview me if you take me with you for the other inter-views — *all* of them."

"I'll do without your interview," I said through clenched teeth.

"Then you won't be a good reporter! You'll be a fake . . . "

I tried leaving the room. Roger followed me, yelling, "Your article needs me. Do you want to be a fake? It won't be balanced!"

"All right!" I gave in after he followed me into the bathroom.

We settled on the frayed living room couch, me with my pencil and notepad. I cleared my throat. "Roger Hadley, how will this move affect you?"

Roger looked blank. "You already know this stuff."

"I have to ask you for a quote. That's how it works."

"Oh. Okay. I'm a detective investigating the bizarre, see? And I'm on this big case — the Mystery of Mr. Wooley. And if I have to move I'll never solve it and the world won't be a safe place."

"I can't write that!" I said, getting up.

"Why not?"

"Just leave Mr. Wooley out of it."

"Okay, okay. Ask me again."

"Roger Hadley, how do you feel about being evicted?"

"Mad, really mad. I mean, Mr. Dutton said we could live here for years, and now he's throwing us out. And I didn't even break anything. Well, nothing big."

" 'Mad, really mad.' Check."

"Check what?" Roger said.

"That's what reporters say. It means I have your quote."

"Oh. And I like it here. The school's pretty good, and I'm starting to make friends. And there aren't any aunts."

" 'No aunts.' Check." BOY IS OUTRAGED. "Now where's Emma?"

She wasn't in her room. She wasn't stuffing her face in the kitchen.

"Emma! Where are you?" I started to feel alarmed. I was supposed to be baby-sitting her, and she was lost. "Emma, I have Oreos."

Roger even got off the couch to help me look for her. We finally found her hiding way up on the top shelf of her closet. She had climbed up a stack of toys, and they had fallen down.

"I'm staying here with Winson forever. We'll never move," she said.

"You can't stay there forever. You'll have to get down to go to the bathroom," I said.

"I'll never go to the bathroom again."

"You'll have to come down to eat."

"I'll never eat again."

I showed her the Oreos.

"I might come down just for a minute."

When she was settled on the couch with a fistful of cookies I said to her, "Emma, tell me how you feel about moving."

"Ask Winson first."

I looked at the ceiling. "All right. Winston, does it bother you, having to move?"

"Winson says she won't move, no matter what. Because this is home, and none of the other places were."

"I see," I said, writing very quickly.

"And when you move all the rooms are wrong."

" 'Wrong. The rooms are wrong.' And what about you, Emma?"

"Same thing."

"I see." DESPERATE CHILD SUFFERS SOMETHING BECAUSE OF MOVE. "I'll work on it." I got out an old camera that still had film in it. "Okay. Now I take your pictures."

"Can Winson stand beside me?" Emma asked.

"Yes. Roger, take your finger out of your nose and stop crossing your eyes. Were you born like the rest of us or did you crawl out from under a rock?" Roger poked me. "Stop being a pill, Roger, or you won't be in the picture at all!"

I snapped three pictures. In the first one Roger hung an arm over his head and drooled. In the second one he pretended to choke himself. In the third one he leered and growled, "Dutton is a creep!"

"I'm leaving now," I said. "Emma, you have to come with me. Roger isn't old enough or normal enough to baby-sit you."

"Thank you," Roger said.

"I'm not going anywhere without Winson!" Emma said.

"Winston can come too. I'm going to interview the other tenants."

"Hey!" Roger said. "You promised I could come too!"

"That was before you poked me."

"I'll tell everyone you're a fake."

"All right! We'll all go, but I'm the only one who gets to talk. I'm the reporter. Come on."

LANEY'S LAW NUMBER 38:
Antarctica isn't far enough away. Even outer space is too close for little brothers and sisters.

Chapter 4

"I cannot believe what Dutton is doing. He is an unconscionable man!"

Miss Applebaum was willing to give me quotes — lots of them. Her hair was orange today. She poked and prodded the air around her as she spoke. In her right hand was a paintbrush with orangy-red paint on it, and spatters of paint hit her face and her smock as she gestured.

Roger nodded eagerly. "Mr. Dutton is a slug."

"An unusual word, but one not without its merits," Miss Applebaum said, her eyes crinkling at the corners.

I poked Roger with my elbow. "I'm writing an article about Mr. Dutton, Miss Applebaum. Can I interview you?"

"Certainly. I do so admire you for leaping into the fray. Come in, all of you."

"Er, thank you, but Mom says we shouldn't go into strangers' homes."

"A sensible precaution. An admirable woman, your mother. I wish I had taken more time to get to know her, but one becomes so caught up in one's own pursuits. You comprehend?"

"Er, yes," I said. "You said the other day you were going to take Mr. Dutton to court."

"Yes. So far I have attempted to communicate telephonically with my nephew Thornton no less than twelve times! He is a lawyer. There seems to be something wrong with his infernal machine."

"His — "

"Telephone answering machine. I have never trusted such gadgets. They are prone to breakdown at the most inopportune moments. One is so much safer communicating face to face, or at least voice to voice."

"Except when you're talking to a slug," Roger said.

"Hm. But I will not allow such setbacks to prevent me from pursuing the wrongful eviction suit!" Miss Applebaum said. "I have a secret weapon, you see — Thornton's mother's telephone number! If forced, I shall employ it without mercy."

Roger looked puzzled, but he said "slug" again anyway.

"So you are determined to fight Mr. Dutton?" I asked Miss Applebaum.

"Exactly so! He has low morals. You are children of remarkable perspicacity. I am surprised I did not notice it before."

Emma was watching Miss Applebaum closely.

"How long have you lived here?" I asked.

Miss Applebaum's expression softened. "Longer than one cares to admit, my child. Shall we say, about fifteen years? After the first five years I began to arrange it as I like. Now," she paused, "*no one* will separate me from it!"

"TENANT PREPARED TO FIGHT," I said, scribbling.

"Precisely!" As Miss Applebaum gestured, paint flew into her hair.

Emma pulled at the hem of Miss Applebaum's pinkish-red smock. "How do you get your hair that colour?" she asked.

Miss Applebaum put back her head and laughed. She sounded like a bell. "That, my dear child, shall remain my secret!"

She winked and closed the door.

Emma grinned. "Winson likes her."

Roger quivered with excitement as we climbed the stairs to the second floor. "At last I'll see Mr. Wooley! It won't mean much if we have to knock — he'll have time to hide things, or maybe change the way he looks," he muttered. "But it will be better than nothing."

At Mr. Wooley's door we all stood a moment, hesitating.

"If Mr. Wooley hasn't got any face, you shouldn't scream or anything, Emma," Roger whispered.

"What?" Emma squeaked.

"I mean, he might have a terrible vitamin disease, from eating nothing but olives for a zillion years, and it might have rotted his face off, and maybe that's why he doesn't go out."

"You're scaring Winson," Emma whined.

"Roger," I said, "shut up!" I knocked on the door. We waited. And waited. "Maybe he isn't home."

"He's *always* home," Roger said.

I knocked again.

The doorknob rattled. A thin, shaky voice came from inside the apartment. "Who's there?" it called.

"It's Laney, Roger and Emma from upstairs," I called back.

"Wh—what do you want?"

"We don't want to move. We're trying to stop Mr. Dutton. Can we talk to you please?"

There was the sound of a chain. The doorknob turned.

"He's coming! He's coming!" Roger hissed.

The door opened part way and a very old face appeared.

Mr. Wooley was almost bald. Bits of white hair clung to his round head. He blinked at us with watery blue eyes through thick glasses.

"You've heard the news?" I asked him. "About Mr.

Dutton throwing us out of the house?"

Mr. Wooley nodded once. He was wearing a very old grey sweater. It was buttoned wrong.

"Do you have any ideas about that?" That wasn't what I meant to say. I kept trying to see more of Mr. Wooley, and I couldn't think straight. His pants were baggy and his slippers had holes in the toes. He looked as if he had been assembled quickly, and some parts had been left out. His vague eyes seemed to be looking for the missing parts. In the corner next to the door was a green umbrella.

"I don't have any ideas," he said in his quavering voice.

"Can we come in?" Roger asked. He was craning forward, trying to see past Mr. Wooley into the apartment.

"Come — ?" Mr. Wooley's chin trembled.

"Why is your sweater buttoned wrong?" Emma asked.

Mr. Wooley's eyes fastened on her.

"Winson wants to know," Emma said.

"W–Winson?" Mr. Wooley's eyes travelled over us and over the hall beyond.

"This is my friend Winson." Emma indicated the air beside her.

"Oh." Mr. Wooley blinked.

"Winson doesn't want to move."

"Oh." Mr. Wooley looked sad. "Neither do I. But — " He suddenly looked worried. His eyes flitted about.

"I like your umbrella," Emma said.

"Do you? It has birds."

Emma frowned. "Umbrellas don't have birds."

Mr. Wooley smiled. "Th–this one does," he said shyly. He handed it to Emma. "Go ahead. Open it up."

"If we can come in — " Roger started pushing on the door. "You know, come in for a second and talk about not wanting to move, and birdcages, and UFOs."

I poked Roger.

Mr. Wooley began to blink rapidly. "I, I have to go now."

"But your umbrella — " I said.

The door closed. "L–leave it by the door."

"But you haven't told me how you feel about moving," I called.

"Sorry," came the soft reply. "Very, very sorry."

"How long have you lived here?" I called.

There were shuffling sounds behind the door, but no reply. Mr. Wooley was gone.

"I don't have enough quotes. This is your fault, Roger! You shouldn't have pushed on the door."

"But I couldn't *see* anything."

"We saw Mr. Wooley. He's an ordinary old man," I said. I tried out a headline: SENIOR CITIZEN SHATTERED BY EVICTION.

"Wow!" Emma said, opening the umbrella.

It did have birds — painted yellow and white birds flying all over a green background, and a handle that looked sort of like bamboo cane, with a bird's head where the handle usually is. I helped Emma close it again. "This isn't your umbrella. We'll leave it here."

"I tell you, he's hiding something," Roger said. "Otherwise, why wouldn't he open the door up? Why wouldn't he let us come in? Mr. Wooley *is* a real live mystery! I knew it."

Chapter 5

[November 17 — Wednesday]

Finished my article today during study period when I was supposed to be working on Science. Actually, I think the article's pretty good. It answers all the Who?, What?, When?, Where? and Why? questions World Famous Reporters are supposed to answer.

It's a good thing I plan to be a reporter, because there's a good chance I'm going to fail Science this term. I haven't redone my graph yet, but I don't care anymore. Why should World Famous Reporters have to worry about science anyway?

I am writing my article in my journal so I will always have a copy of my first big success.

CHILDREN AND SENIOR CITIZENS
THROWN INTO STREET

The tenants of 54 Hogart Street are being evicted by their landlord, Mr. Dutton, for no good reason, so he can make a lot of money.

Widowed mother of three innocent children, Anne Hadley, said, "Mr. Dutton spoke of our living here for years. I didn't know he could kick us out." Mrs. Hadley is searching for another home for her family. If she can't find one, the family will be divided up among their aged aunts.

Outraged Roger Hadley, nine, said Mr. Dutton made him, "Mad, real mad!" Desperate Emma Hadley, five, said this apartment "Feels like home." She may be having adjustment problems.

Another tenant, determined Miss Applebaum, plans to sue Mr. Dutton for wrongful eviction. "Dutton has low morals," she said.

The last tenant, old Mr. Wooley, was close to tears when interviewed, and had buttoned his sweater wrong.

Should Mr. Dutton be able to get away with it? I don't think so!

Respectfully, Elaine Hadley
(Pictures of Outraged and Desperate Children Enclosed)

Roger trapped me as I headed for the newspaper office after school.

"I'm going with you," he said.

"No you're not!"

"If you don't let me come I'll tell Mom about your article!"

"No deal! You're a troublemaker."

"No, I'm not."

"You push on doors and you can't keep your mouth shut. You stay here."

"Do you really think Mom will let you say your sister has adjustment problems? And what does that mean, anyway?"

"How do you know I said that? You've been reading my journal again, you rat!"

"If you leave me here, Mom may force me to tell, and she'll stop you and you'll never become a World Famous Reporter!"

"I hate you, Roger! All right, come. But if you say one word I'll throttle you! You are the worst brother in the world."

Roger grinned. "Thank you."

The *Daily News* office is only a few streetcar stops away. Mom lets us travel on the streetcar during the day if we stay together. Roger and I got there quickly. There was a receptionist at the main desk.

"A special delivery for the newsroom," I told her. "Rush!"

"Fifth floor," she said, smiling.

In the elevator we could see our faces in the shiny

metal walls. Roger folded both arms around his head and turned his lower lip inside out.

"Roger," I said. "Grow up!"

He stuck his tongue out. "You're just jealous 'cause you can't do this!"

A woman got on the elevator at the third floor and quickly got off again.

"I'm good!" Roger said, grinning.

"You're revolting!"

"Thank you. I know why you won't let me tell Mom about this. You're afraid it won't work!"

My face turned red. "I am absolutely, a million per cent, completely, totally sure this will work!" I said.

"Hah!" Roger said. He looked thoughtful. "Maybe the newspaper would be interested in knowing about a man with a ginormous secret."

"This trip is for *my* article!" I said. "Say a word, say a single word about UFOs or aliens and I'll — "

The doors opened at the fifth floor. The hallway was carpeted, in green with grey flecks, so I didn't hear our footsteps. At the end of the hall was a room filled with desks and busy people and computers. A real newsroom! But there was also another receptionist, blocking our way. Her hair was very long and black. My hands felt slippery.

"Special delivery for the news editor," I said. "Rush!" (I saw this in a movie once.)

"I'll take it," she said, holding out her hand. Her nail polish was blue.

I gripped my article tightly. "I have to deliver it in person."

"Do you have an appointment?" she asked.

"Er — "

"Of course we do!" Roger said.

"With whom?"

Roger poked me. "I *told* you to write down his name, Laney! With — you know — what's his name."

The woman smiled. Her lipstick was a funny colour too. "Nice try, kids. Don't get lost in the elevator going down."

"But you have to let us in," Roger cried. "It's a matter of life and death!" He squeezed a tear out of one eye. "Really!"

"Sure. If I let in every kid who tried to gate-crash, we'd never get any work done."

"And maybe, just maybe, you'd miss a huge story," Roger said.

"Oh yeah? Tell me about it."

"There's this man hiding out in our apartment house," Roger said, his eyes bugging out with excitement. "I think he may be an alien."

I nudged Roger. "Don't listen to him. We're being evicted, and we think maybe it's against the law, but we can't afford to hire a lawyer, and my sister's starting to crack up because of it, and we don't have a dad, and this old man who never comes out — he's being evicted too, and there's a lady named Applebaum who says Dutton has low morals, and she's going to sue . . . "

"Hey, Petrie, we've got a live one!" the woman called.

A tall thin red-headed woman came over to us. Her hair was cut short and she was dressed in blue pants and shirt, with a white bow tie. "Make my day, Mai-Lin," she said.

"Well go on, kid," the receptionist said to me. "Give it to her."

"Are you the editor?" I asked.

The woman grinned. "Not yet. I'm one of the junior reporters on roadblock duty. What's your story? A school project?"

"No!" I handed her my article, which had gotten creased by then, I can't remember how, and told her what I had told Mai-Lin, or tried to.

Roger interrupted. "But there's an even bigger story! This man in our apartment house never comes out! He's either an alien or a mad scientist. Maybe he was kidnapped by aliens, so he's afraid to go out, see?"

"Good one!" Petrie said, smiling.

"Shut up, Roger!" I shoved him.

"That's quite a story, kids." The smile became a grin.

"I'm not with him!" I said. "He reads stupid comics. We really are being evicted and it isn't fair."

"Right." She didn't even look at my article. "Has anyone been arrested?"

"Er, no."

"Who is this lawyer? Where has he filed the suit?"

"Um, he hasn't yet. He's Thorn-something. But he will!"

"Sure, kid. Listen. Hundreds of people are evicted every month in a city of this size. This isn't newsworthy. There's no drama or excitement to set the story apart, though I do like the part about the aliens. Come see us in another ten years."

She smiled as she handed the envelope back. It was a kind smile.

"Oh yeah?" Roger said. "Well I think you couldn't tell a story from the nose on your face. You stink!"

"Thank you," Petrie said.

Roger blinked.

I couldn't sit on Roger in the elevator, because there were people on it, so I yelled instead. "Aliens! You told them we had a story about aliens! I'm going to throttle you, Roger!" JURY AWARDS GIRL FOR THROTTLING WALKING DISASTER ZONE CALLED ROGER.

"I was just trying to get their interest."

"You made them laugh at us!"

"I made them listen to us. They weren't even going to listen at first."

"You make me so mad — " I couldn't think of anything else to say until we were at the streetcar stop. Even then, I was only talking to Roger because there wasn't a real human around. "Newspapers are supposed to be the voice of the Little People. Mr. Wyman says so. If we aren't little enough, I don't know who is!"

LANEY'S LAW NUMBER 39:
Teacher's don't know everything.
Why do they sound like they do?

Roger didn't say anything, so I just kept going. "Mr. Wyman says newspapers are supposed to be the champion of the underdog! Well what do you think *we* are?"

"Hey! Who are you calling a dog?" Roger asked.

"Don't say anything! Don't speak to me again, ever!"

When we got home I locked myself in the bathroom and flushed the toilet a lot.

There weren't going to be any headlines. No headlines at all. And no World Famous Reporter either.

Mom came to the door. "Laney, what's wrong?" I wouldn't come out. Emma said Winson had to go really bad. I told her to go somewhere else. Then Mom said, "The news is starting in two minutes. I hear there's been a riot."

LANEY'S LAW NUMBER 40:
The news always comes first.

Mom handed me my dinner. Emma let me sit on Winston's chair. Roger stayed out of throttling distance, a dog-eared copy of *True Tales* clutched in his hands.

"Writing an article was a wonderful idea," Mom told me. "I'm very proud of you for doing it, Laney. But sometimes you just can't change things, no matter how much you want to."

"Roger promised not to tell you!" I said.

"When you wouldn't come out of the bathroom Mom squeezed it out of me!" Roger cried. "It's not my fault."

"Nothing's ever your fault!" I snapped.

Roger thought a minute. "That's true."

There wasn't any riot on the news, just a protest. A bunch of people carrying signs marched in front of City Hall. An old building was being torn down, and they were protesting. Newspeople with cameras were everywhere. Sure, I thought, you'll cover a protest over a stupid building, but you won't cover people being thrown out of their home!

One of the protesters started throwing rocks, and police officers moved from the sidelines to arrest him. Reporters pushed forward to get his comments. "This city doesn't care about its history!" he said. "Well, I'll make them care!"

All of a sudden I felt much better.

"Laney, I have some appointments to see apartments, but I won't go if you don't feel like babysitting," Mom said.

"I'm okay, Mom. You can go."

Mom chewed her lower lip. "If we had more time — "

"Go ahead, Mom. Really."

Mom ruffled my hair and kissed me on the forehead. She hadn't done that for a long time.

"You're standing in front of the TV, Mom!" I said. "The news is still on and I can't see. Are you going or not?"

Mom laughed. "I'm going. I won't be late. Do your homework."

"Winson doesn't have any homework," Emma said.

"Then she can help you with yours," Mom said.

Emma smiled. "Okay."

Just before Mom left Miss Applebaum knocked on our door, her arms full of freshly baked cookies. "Mrs. Hadley, what gems you have as children, what treasures! May I come in?"

"Certainly. Please call me Anne."

"I should have visited you long ago. I blame myself. I baked these for your treasures. I hope you don't mind." Miss Applebaum swept into the apartment like a small cyclone and placed the tray of cookies on the kitchen table. She was wearing a big purple apron. "To think of these children mobilizing against Mr. Dutton! You must be so proud of them."

Mom smiled. "I am, Miss Applebaum."

"Please call me Victoria."

"Unfortunately, Victoria, the newspaper won't print Elaine's article."

"A short-sighted move on the part of the *Daily News!*" Miss Applebaum snorted. "Do not despair, children. There is still my suit!"

"So you really are suing Mr. Dutton?"

"I am! I have successfully placed a message on my nephew Thornton's infernal machine. One expects a reply momentarily. I must go. Do not abandon hope, children. Together we will defeat Mr. Dutton! If there is anything I can do, do not hesitate to ask." She smiled at Mom. "Please join me for tea at your convenience."

After she had left Roger said, "I'm a treasure." He grinned. "Maybe Miss Applebaum's going to stop the slug."

"Yeah, like the newspaper helped *us*," I said.

"Oh." Roger's face fell. "But we don't have any more ideas. Think, Laney. Think!"

"Quiet, Roger," I said. "I need to watch this."

I finished my macaroni and cheese and green beans without noticing I had eaten beans. After the "riot" coverage there was some political news, and then the newscaster talked about a murder. Mom usually turns off this kind of news, but she had already gone.

"I'll never find out about Mr. Wooley now!" Roger moaned.

"There's nothing to find out," I said.

"Yes there is, Laney. If he's not an alien he could be a criminal mastermind, hiding here for years. But we'll never know. We'll be living way out in the east end!"

"Winson and me won't move!" Emma said. "Why don't you hear me?"

"We heard you, Emma," I said. "You and Winston won't move."

"Yeah!" she said.

"There has to be a way!" Roger groaned. "What about . . . Now there's an idea!" Roger looked at the murder story with a ferocious grin. "Who cares about the power of the press when you know someone who has a pet tarantula!"

"Who has one?" Emma asked.

"Speedo Morgan. He's in my class. I wonder if he'd loan it to me . . . "

"You can't murder Mr. Dutton," I told him.

"Why not? He's a home-snatcher! A slug! It's a perfect plan! He's bringing some possible investors to the house tomorrow night. Mom told us while you were in the bathroom."

"Why investors? Do you suppose he needs people to put money into the house?"

"What do I care? Mom says they would help pay for renovations. But we would already be gone!"

"Wait a minute. Did you say he's showing the house tomorrow night?"

"Yeah, then again Saturday morning at ten o'clock. But never mind all that. The thing is, Dutton's coming here, and we've got to stop him. So I'll put the tarantula down Disgusting Dutton's shirt when he comes. Nobody could blame me for what a spider does!"

Emma had been following this conversation with interest. "Winson thinks it's a good idea," she said.

"Don't you think someone would notice a tarantula at the scene of the crime, and wonder how it got down Dutton's shirt? Besides, I think a grown man could survive a tarantula bite."

Roger looked disappointed, and then excited again. "Okay, we'll wait until he's under our landing and we'll poke that loose chunk of plaster so it falls on Dutton's foot!"

"No, Roger. No, Emma. No spiders or accidents

with parts of the house. You can't hurt Mr. Dutton. Hurting people is wrong! And Mom wouldn't like visiting you in prison."

"I suppose you have a better idea!"

"If I did, I wouldn't tell you. You'd just ruin it, the way you ruined my article! And you'd blab to Mom."

"You're so unfair! I swear I won't say a word!"

"Forget it, Roger!"

"But I'll help!"

"Your kind of help I can do without! Look at what you did at the *Daily News*, you and your aliens!"

LANEY'S LAW NUMBER 41:
Never, never, NEVER tell Roger anything!

"Yeah, well if you won't tell me your idea, I won't tell you my even better idea."

"What's that?"

"It's a secret."

"Fine!"

I went in search of some Bristol board left over from my last Geography project. I made Roger swear to watch Emma.

"Why? Where are you going? I want to come with you," he said.

"No deal! You stay here. I'll be right back."

I ran downstairs to see Miss Applebaum. She smiled as she opened her door. I told her my plan.

"Superb!" she said. "Wait until Mr. Dutton sees us! I am gratified to be included in your plan, Elaine, especially since my nephew Thornton is still evading me! How can one help? Will you need cookies? No. This calls for something better! What else is required?"

"Maybe I can get Mr. Wooley to help us too."

"I do not think so. One tried to befriend Mr. Wooley when one first moved in. He will come to the door, of course, but he won't come out, and I never managed to get in."

Miss Applebaum turned out to be right. Mr. Wooley's reaction was different from hers. "Oh, no!" he said, paling. "I, I couldn't! I, I have to go now."

Two buttons were missing from his sweater and his socks didn't match. I hadn't really counted on him.

Chapter 6

[November 18 — Thursday]

Horrible day at school. Mr. Wyman asked where my graph was. I had to tell him what happened. He said the rules would not be changed because of brothers or sisters.

Roger slumped and glowered at dinner. Mom lost her temper. Then she apologized. "I'm sorry. We're all tired and none of us is looking forward to moving."

Emma muttered, "I'm staying here with Winson!"

"Would you really want to stay here without the rest of us?" Mom asked. "Even Winston might not want to do that."

Emma thought. "Yes, she would."

"Well! Time to do the dishes. Mr. Dutton will be here soon. I want you all on your best behaviour."

Roger moved a chair close to the window so he could read bizarre stories with his feet on the window ledge. Emma managed to climb from that chair to the mantlepiece while we were doing the dishes. There are big plaster roses the size of fists stuck on the wall above the mantlepiece — a whole row of them. Some of the petals are chipped. Emma played with them, muttering, "Home." Mom lifted her down and pushed the heavy chair back.

Dutton showed two women out of his car and into the house. I watched them from the window. Then I went out onto the landing. Dutton's loud voice carried from the entrance far below.

"As you can see, the house is in excellent condition, from a vintage period. Very little investment would be required to turn it into condominiums. Look at this original woodwork."

"Hmm. This hallway needs replastering." This voice was uncertain.

"Perhaps, but when the structure of a building is as sound as this one, it merits additional investment."

The voices grew indistinct as Dutton and his investors entered Miss Applebaum's apartment. Not long after, they reappeared on the stairs and climbed to Mr. Wooley's. Someone was whistling down below. Roger!

"What are you doing here?" Dutton asked Roger, who was lurking by Mr. Wooley's door.

"Just passing by," Roger said.

"Pass, then."

Roger muttered as he climbed the stairs and raced to the railing beside me, "Get out of the way. I can't see anything."

I caught a glimpse of Mr. Wooley's miserable face below as Dutton waved the women inside.

"Pay no attention to the tenants and their things," Dutton said crisply. "I'll have them out of here by the fifteenth of December."

"That would be acceptable."

"Slug!" Roger snapped. He eyed the loose plaster.

Mom found us peering over the railing. "All right, you two. Inside," she said.

Roger disappeared.

Dutton's voice carried from the stairwell. "Condominiums are easier to manage, of course." Then he was at our door.

Mom gave him a polite but chilly look as she let him in. He showed off the "original period fireplace, with its ornate plaster moulding in the shape of roses" in our living room.

One of the women nodded. "From a purely business point of view the property has merit."

Mom's face was blank as she shooed me out of the hallway.

"What about those cracks in the ceiling above the fireplace?" one of the women asked.

"Mom! Mo-om! The pipes have burst again!" Roger bellowed.

He came hurtling down the hallway from the bathroom. Water flew from him in all directions. He was carrying a bucket full of it. Before anyone could stop him he tripped and emptied it over Dutton and the investors.

HUMAN WRECKING BALL STRIKES AGAIN!

"My clothes are ruined!" one of the women cried.

The other woman opened her mouth and closed it, like a fish, saying nothing but, "Oh! Oh!"

"Mrs. Hadley," Dutton roared. "Restrain your children!"

"Children are not animals," Mom said. "They cannot be restrained. Accidents sometimes happen! I'll get you all towels."

"This was no accident, Mrs. Hadley! What do you take me for? I hold you responsible for any water damage."

Mom nodded curtly. "Very well."

One of the women whirled around to face Dutton. "You distinctly told us the plumbing was in perfect working order."

"I assure you it is. This is a juvenile prank, meant to discredit the property. Surely you can see that!"

The woman's eyes searched Dutton's face. "I would like to go. I'm not sure of anything right now."

The women left.

LANEY'S LAW NUMBER 42:
Even people with a lot of money can be smart.

58

Mr. Dutton glared at us. "You are interfering in my legal rights, and I won't have it. I've had very little to do with children in my life, but even I know the difference between accidents and sabotage! It was a mistake letting you move in here in the first place. I cannot tolerate disruption. Have I made myself clear?"

"Perfectly," Mom said. Her face was very pale.

Mr. Dutton left.

Mom handed Roger a mop. "We may not like Mr. Dutton, but there is to be no repetition of that performance! You can't lash out at people you don't like, Roger. That is no solution."

"But Mom!"

"Promise me there will be no more attacks on Mr. Dutton — no water balloons, no squirt guns, no lies about the plumbing or anything else. Do you promise?"

"Yes," Roger growled.

"Come on." Mom sighed. "I'll help you mop up."

Chapter 7

[November 19 — Friday]

Found Roger lowering himself from his bedroom window, on a rope made from torn bed sheets.

"One more move and you will move out, permanently!" I said.

I hauled him back inside. He hadn't gotten very far.

"I've *got* to see Mr. Wooley's secret," he moaned. "I've *got* to know!" Then he looked down. "The ground's a long way away, isn't it?"

"You'd better think about what to tell Mom about her sheets."

"But they were the only things the right size! Laney, you're planning something. Please say you are. Mom wants us to start packing! She brought home cardboard boxes today."

"Goodbye, Roger."

I closed the window, locked it and confiscated the bed-sheet rope.

Mom went to Miss Applebaum's for tea and pronounced her an eccentric but nice woman.

"What's that mean?" Emma asked.

"She's not like anybody else. Come on, Emma. It's time to start packing."

"I won't pack!"

Emma managed to climb onto the top of the fridge and stayed there for a whole hour. Six Oreos were needed to get her down.

"All right, Muffin," Mom said, "you don't have to pack."

Mom hadn't called Emma that since she was two. Emma seemed to be getting younger every day. At night Mom snuck into her room and started packing old toys.

"It's the aunts, isn't it?" Roger asked gloomily, kicking a chair.

"Not necessarily," Mom said. "There are still weeks left."

"It's the aunts."

[November 20 — Saturday]

A sunny fall day. Perfect.

Mom asked Miss Applebaum to keep an eye on us, made us all promise to be polite and went out

61

to check a "good prospect" on the east side.

Miss Applebaum appeared at our door in an orange dress. Her hair was red again. Her cheeks were pink. She brought triple-chocolate brownies ("for strength") and five signs in really bright colours. The signs read Don't Sell Our Home, Unfairly Evicted, Landlord Breaks Promise, Children Thrown into Street and Give Me Freedom or Give Me Death. I'm not sure how the last one fit in, but it sounded good. "When I was young we were always protesting," she said.

I had my notebook and my camera ready. There was no way to keep Roger away now, so I handed him a sign as we all trooped down to the street.

"I *knew* you were planning something! Laney, you're almost smart! What about Mr. Wooley? Did you ask him?"

I nodded. "He said he couldn't come."

"What is he hiding?" Roger cried.

"He's not hiding anything, Roger. He's just shy."

"I take it back. You're not smart, Laney." He checked his sign. "Hey, I don't want this sign. I want the Give Me Death one."

"What a surprise."

"Me too! I want a sign!" Emma cried. She had on her yellow coat.

Miss Applebaum handed her Children Thrown into Street. She had made it smaller than the other signs.

"You are a superior protester!" Miss Applebaum said.

"What about a sign for Winson?"

I had briefed Miss Applebaum on Winston.

"She can help you."

The curtains at one of the second-floor windows twitched.

I could think of a lot of good headlines. CHILD SENDS DESPERATE PLEA FOR HELP. PROTEST ON HOGART STREET SHAKES NEIGHBOURHOOD.

So my story hadn't been dramatic enough, eh? Not newsworthy? Well, I'd give them newsworthy!

I took Don't Sell Our Home and started marching up and down the sidewalk. It was almost ten o'clock.

Mr. Trumpkin was out raking leaves. "What's this?" he asked, coming over.

"This, sir, is a Protest!" Miss Applebaum said. "A cry for justice! Would you care to join us?"

He frowned. "Is this legal?"

"Absolutely. I checked with my nephew Thornton. He's a lawyer."

"Hmph." Mr. Trumpkin went back to raking.

Two people across the street pointed at us and called to neighbours. Some people walked over to ask what was happening.

"Mr. Dutton is unfairly evicting us from our home!" Miss Applebaum said. She chopped the air with her hands.

"Gee. That's rough," a girl said. She had the longest braids I'd ever seen, and crooked teeth. She picked up Unfairly Evicted. "My name is Anastasia," she said, adding, "My mother watches too many movies. I live over there." She pointed across the street. "Glad to meet you."

She put out her hand. Roger looked at it.

"I'm Roger. What do you mean about movies?" he asked.

"Would *you* like to be named Anastasia?"

Roger shrugged. "Why not? How do you keep your braids from getting in your dinner?"

They marched together for awhile, until a man in a brown coat asked them to get out of the way. "Oh, yeah?" Roger said. "Oh, yeah?" The man crossed to the other side of the street and walked past.

Roger started to run after him. I grabbed him as a car whizzed past. "Roger, getting yourself killed isn't part of the plan!"

"Hah!"

"Just don't ruin my plan this time! Don't interfere!"

"Who's interfering? I'm helping!"

I went back to keeping a close eye on Emma.

Miss Applebaum organized a chant.

"Oh no! We won't go!" she shouted. "All together now!"

"Oh no! We won't go! Oh no! We won't go!"

Miss Applebaum was fantastic!

LANEY'S LAW NUMBER 43:
Eccentric is a good thing.

Emma caught on to the chant right away. Her blond curls bobbed up and down as she yelled. Roger shouted loud enough to be heard in Antarctica. Anastasia grinned and joined in. Doors opened all along the street. Heads poked out to see what the noise was about. Some more people wandered over.

"That's it!" I said. "I'm phoning the *Daily News*. They've got to cover this!" PEACEFUL DEMONSTRATORS WIN HEARTS OF THE CITY. "Miss Applebaum, watch Emma, please."

I rushed in and used Miss Applebaum's phone. She had left her door unlocked "for just that noble purpose."

For a second I got stalled looking at Miss Applebaum's apartment. All her walls were covered with paintings of flowers. This must be what she meant by "arranging things" the way she liked. No wonder Mom had called her eccentric! Then I picked up the phone. I had written the number on my hand.

"Daily News," a bored voice answered me.

"You've got to see this! There's a protest on Hogart Street!"

"What? On what street?"

I spelled the name of the street.

"Hey, kid, who are you? Is this some kind of a joke?"

"No joke! I've gotta go. It's turning into a riot!"

The last thing I heard was the voice on the phone shouting, "Does anyone know anything about Hogart Street?"

I hung up the phone and ran outside. The crowd was bigger. Emma was sitting on the lawn.

"So why is he kicking you out?" someone yelled.

"The unprincipled landlord wishes to turn this house into condominiums," Miss Applebaum said. "We are being evicted!"

"That doesn't seem fair."

There were a lot of people standing watching the protest now.

"I'm tired," Emma said. "I'm going in."

"Just stay for a little while longer," I said.

The crowd was mixed — grandmothers, teen-agers, men in overalls, women in jogging suits, a delivery boy on a bicycle, two boys with safety pins in their ears.

"Oh no. We won't go! Oh no. We won't go!"

Boy, are we loud, I thought. "It's working!"

At that moment Mr. Dutton's car pulled up to the curb. He got out of the driver's seat and stared at the protest.

A man and a woman got out of the car and looked at Dutton. They were wearing grey suits, even the woman. Dutton circled around the protesters and waved his investors toward the house.

"This is outrageous!" Dutton had to shout to be heard above the chant. "Pay no attention to this disorder, Mr. Whitney, Mrs. Gambini!"

"This is the fink who's throwing us out," Roger yelled. Dutton dodged as Roger approached.

"You're evicting children?" Mrs. Gambini asked. "I thought you said they were seniors, ready for a nursing home."

"Most of them are. This is business. You understand."

"I do not!" Mrs. Gambini said. "I won't be part of this kind of an eviction." She slipped out of Dutton's grasp.

"I have to agree with Mrs. Gambini," Mr. Whitney said, retreating to the car.

"But wait — "

"Dutton's nothing but a really tall slug!" Roger yelled. He waved his sign in Mr. Dutton's face.

Dutton swept the sign aside, just as Roger bobbed closer. The corner of the sign grazed Roger's face.

"Hey!" He poked Dutton.

Dutton pushed his hand away.

"Hey!"

"No, Roger!" I yelled. I threw down my sign and ran. There were still a lot of people between me and Roger.

Roger threw himself at Dutton. I threw myself at Roger, trying to stop him.

I'm not quite sure what happened next. Dutton seemed to rush toward my fist. Or maybe my fist rushed toward him. I remember yelling, "Leave my brother alone!" and a sharp pain in my hand as it connected with Dutton's face.

Then Roger and I were on the ground. Roger grabbed Dutton's leg.

Dutton struggled for an instant. "Let go!"

A big shoe swept toward us.

An outraged shout split the air. "Stop that, you, you — "

I looked up to see Miss Applebaum shove Dutton out of the way.

Dutton turned purple. He snatched a cellular phone from his pocket and punched in 9-1-1. "Get me the police!" he shouted.

I saw a streak of yellow next to me. Emma had gotten through somehow and had latched onto Dutton's ankles. It was hard to tell whose ankles were whose for awhile. The sound of a siren came before I had them sorted out. Two new pairs of ankles came into the picture, and a loud voice said, "Okay, break it up."

A huge man and a woman belonged to the new ankles. They wore police uniforms. It was like looking up at big blue refrigerators.

"Get them off me!" Dutton said.

Then something flashed behind me. Petrie stood there snapping pictures.

"Say cheese," Petrie told Dutton. "I'm from the *Daily News*."

Chapter 8

"I want to charge them! That's what I want to do! There must be something I can charge them with!" Dutton's eyes were still spitting fire.

The policeman arched his brows. They were bushy brows, matching his thatch of thick brown-grey hair and his creased face. He had given his name as Officer Warren. "I see. The children are all young, you understand."

"What do I care about their ages? They are juvenile delinquents and I want them charged."

CHILDREN ROT IN JAIL, I thought.

Officer Warren took a sip from his coffee cup. We

sat in our living room while he filled out forms. Mom stood stiffly beside Roger, Emma and me.

"My children are not juvenile delinquents!" Mom said.

I thought at first this was a good sign. Then I saw Mom's face.

"Uh-huh." Officer Warren said.

The other officer was downstairs getting statements from the neighbours. Petrie had taken pictures of them both when they'd separated us from Dutton.

"Well, Mr. Dutton, you can go to a Justice of the Peace and lay a complaint of assault against the oldest child, Elaine. The others are too young to be charged. Elaine is considered old enough to be responsible for her actions."

The officer looked at me. I felt myself go red.

"But all the children attacked me. I want them all charged."

"That isn't possible. That's the law."

"Will Elaine go to jail?" Dutton asked.

Warren shifted in his seat. "That would be up to the judge, sir. But children of that age are not usually sent to jail, no." He looked at us. "On the other hand, Elaine can also charge *you* with assault. I understand blows were exchanged." Officer Warren consulted his notes. "The children claim you struck Elaine's brother in the face with a sign."

"He sure did!" Roger said.

"But that was an accident!"

"And he kicked me too! He's a slug!" Roger hiked up his shirt to show a bruise.

"That looks nasty, son. Was that kick an accident too?" Officer Warren went back to his forms. "Fifty-two-year-old assailant . . . " He measured Mr. Dutton with his eyes. " . . . about one hundred kilograms, struck nine-year-old child of about . . . thirty kilograms . . . " Officer Warren winked at Roger.

"You're making this sound all wrong!" Dutton said. "He attacked me first. *She* punched me in the face!" He pointed to me. Warren squinted at Dutton's face. "There doesn't seem to be any damage. Have you seen a doctor?"

"Of course not, it just happened. And I don't need a doctor! That's not the point."

" . . . although the little girl's hand is sore."

"It's not my fault the girl's hand is sore!"

"Perhaps not."

"You can't let them get away with it! *He* tried to bite my leg." Dutton glared at Roger. "And *she* kicked me!" He pointed at Emma.

Warren looked us over. "Uh-huh. How much do you weigh, er, Emma?"

Emma shrugged. Mom said, "Forty-two pounds."

"About twenty kilograms . . . Uh-*huh*. What the judge might want to know is who started the fight. Who did that?"

Dutton blustered. "He got in my way . . . They were rioting on the street, for goodness sake. Rioting!"

"An interesting turn of phrase. I haven't heard all the statements yet, but the children say the protest was entirely peaceful until you attacked Roger. And then his sister seems to have gotten involved."

I nodded. "I thought he was going to hurt Roger."

The policeman looked at me gravely. "Do you understand that what you did was wrong?"

My voice seemed to be out of order. I nodded again.

LANEY'S LAW NUMBER 44:
Throttling isn't a good idea. Especially when policemen find out about it.

"None of you has ever been in trouble with the law before?"

I shook my head. Mom said, "No."

"Mr. Dutton, from what I've seen and heard, all of you lost your heads a little. You all said and did things you regret — you *and* the children."

"And that hideous woman! Don't forget the woman!"

"The elderly woman. Right. I'm not forgetting her. I understand you're evicting these people, Mr. Dutton. Of course, a landlord has certain rights. But losing a home has an effect on people, especially young, fatherless children and elderly people. I wouldn't be surprised if the judge took that into account."

"But, but you're making it sound . . . " I could see

Dutton's veins. "It sounds as if . . . "

"As if what, Mr. Dutton? As if a healthy adult man beat up on some children? Now I won't be laying charges, but as I said, you can still lay a complaint, *if* a Justice of the Peace is willing to take it. And then Elaine can lay her own complaint. *And* the elderly, frail-looking woman downstairs can do the same. Then, some months from now, at great expense to the taxpayers, you can let a judge decide who was at fault." Officer Warren's eyelids drooped. "But if I were you I would just forget about the whole thing."

"I certainly won't forget about it!" Dutton said.

"Too bad," Officer Warren said. "This could be very unpleasant for all of you." He bent over his forms.

Miss Applebaum came tearing into the room at that moment. "Thornton's here," she panted.

He was at her heels. He looked kind of young for a lawyer, but he had a business card in his hands. "Thornton Brin, Barrister and Solicitor, of Schnoll, Lee and Forbes," he said. "My aunt has asked . . . That is I will be representing the Hadleys in this matter, as well as Miss Applebaum."

"Uh-huh," the policeman said.

"Wow!" Roger said. "We've got a lawyer?"

Thornton straightened his sweatshirt. "If they have been accused of any crime, it will be my privilege to defend them and clear their names."

For a thin guy in a sweatsuit he made good speeches.

"I won't be accusing anyone of anything, but Mr. Dutton has indicated he will be laying complaints against Elaine and Miss Applebaum. Did I tell you, Mr. Dutton, that you may have to prosecute the case yourself if the officers of the court feel, as I do, that this matter isn't worth pursuing?"

Dutton began to sputter. "But, but look at them! They're a landlord's nightmare! They have frightened away four investors!"

"Have they now?" Officer Warren looked sad. "How long do private cases usually take, Mr. Brin?"

"Up to three years. Sometimes more. May I have the name of your lawyer, Mr. Dutton? I will require that information in order to file complaints on behalf of my clients. If you don't have a lawyer yet, I advise you to find one as soon as possible."

Dutton looked like he was going to explode. "You can't, you won't — "

Thornton smiled. "I can. And I will. What complaint is to be made, officer?" The policeman explained. Thornton looked thoughtful. "My clients *might* be willing to forego legal action if no complaints are laid whatsoever, though I would advise them to press for damages. Miss Applebaum has several bruises."

"Damages!" Dutton bellowed.

Thornton took Mom's elbow and whispered in her ear.

"It's amazing how expensive these matters can become once lawyers get involved, you know," Officer

Warren said, shaking his head.

"The name of your lawyer, Mr. Dutton?"

Dutton cursed. "Forget it!" he growled.

"Do I take it you will not press charges in any way, or attempt to wrongfully profit from this incident in the future?" Thornton asked.

"Yes!"

Dutton turned and stalked away.

Roger cheered.

"As for you children," Officer Warren turned stern eyes on us, "you have courage, but fighting isn't the way to use it. The next time I hear about any trouble here I'll charge you myself. Is that clear?" His voice cracked like a whip.

"Yes, sir."

Emma's eyes were the size of saucers. "Will you charge Winson too?"

"Winson?"

Mom whispered something to Officer Warren. His lips twitched. "I will! Winston too! Ma'am, thank you for the coffee." Officer Warren nodded to Mom and got to his feet. "Have you found a new place yet?"

Mom shook her head.

"It's brutal, this recession. Good luck to you. And try to keep your kids off the street."

"I will. Thank you."

Officer Warren winked at Roger again, nodded to the rest of us and headed for the door. Then he paused. "Seems to me I was here once before."

"You were?" Mom looked at us. "Did my children

75

do something else, anything to get in trouble — ?"

Officer Warren laughed. "No, ma'am. Nothing like that. It was a separate case, about twenty years ago. A freak accident, I think. Can't quite recall the details. What was that name? Lambton? Sheeply?" He shrugged. "My memory isn't what it used to be. Mrs. Hadley, if you ever need help, just call. Here's the number of the police station." Then he left.

"I have always liked you, Thornton!" Miss Applebaum said warmly. "From the day I first saw you with your pants around your ankles and a candy cane stuck to your — "

Thornton winced. "Yes. Thank you, Aunt Victoria." He turned to the others. "If you ever need me again, here is my card."

"Thank you very much for coming," Mom said. "But we can't really afford to hire a lawyer. We'll pay you for today of course."

Thornton shook his head. "There will be no charge for today," he said. "I became a lawyer because I wanted to fight men like Dutton, legally. There are too many people like him in this city — people who don't care who they bulldoze on the way to the bank. Landlords aren't all like that, of course. One of my co-workers owns a small apartment building. He would never evict his tenants. What I'm trying to say is I would be happy to represent you for a dollar."

"Oh no," Mom said. "We wouldn't presume to — "

"Besides," Thornton said, with a wry look at

Miss Applebaum, "Great-Aunt Victoria would never forgive me if I did less."

She smiled and nodded. "What a splendid day it has been!" Her face was very pink.

Mom's polite smile didn't reach her eyes. "Victoria, Mr. Brin, would you excuse us for a few minutes?"

"Certainly, my dear," Miss Applebaum said. "I just want you to know how superbly all of your children behaved today. And how very proud one is to know them."

Roger glowed with pleasure.

"Winson likes *you* too," Emma said.

Miss Applebaum beamed. She leaned down and planted a kiss on Emma's hair. Then she democratically kissed Roger and me too.

"Hey," Roger said, squirming away.

"My aunt is difficult to avoid," Thornton said, with a sympathetic look. "I think the Hadleys would like to be alone now," he added, taking Miss Applebaum's elbow.

Being alone proved to be difficult. Anastasia arrived just as Miss Applebaum left.

"Are you guys all right? Do you have criminal records now or anything?"

"No," Roger said, disappointed.

Anastasia spent ten minutes telling Mom how wonderful the protest was.

"I'm sorry you got into trouble because of my children," Mom said.

"Are you kidding? This was the best day of my life! That reporter from the *Daily News* is going to quote me! She said so."

"That's all very well, but — "

The telephone rang. "Oh, hello, Mr. Wooley," Mom said. "Everyone is unharmed, except for a few minor bruises. Thank you for calling."

"Was that Mr. Wooley? We'll go and tell him about it," Roger cried.

"No you won't!" Mom said.

Politely but firmly Mom suggested that it was time for Anastasia to leave.

I did not enjoy the next hour.

"Elaine, I'm surprised at you," Mom began. "This is the sort of stunt I would expect of Roger. You're old enough to know better."

"Protesting is legal — Martin Luther King did it!"

"I do not think Martin Luther King's marches can be compared with the brawl that happened here. You could have hurt Mr. Dutton!"

"Yeah!" Roger said with a grin.

"We have no right to hurt anyone, no matter what we think of him or her! We talked about this before and I thought you understood. You're going to meet lots of people in your life you don't like. They might not like you either! Are you going to get into a fight with all of them?"

"Well . . . "

"*You* could have been hurt! When I saw the police car, well . . . I don't want to lose you. Not any of you!" Mom looked at us. "Don't you ever, ever do anything like that again without telling me in advance! I want each of you to promise."

We did.

"I'm hungry," Emma said.

Mom went to the kitchen to make lunch.

Roger grabbed me by the hand and dragged me back toward the living room.

"Ow! That hand hurts!"

"Oh, yeah. That's your throttling hand. You *wanted* to hit Dutton. Admit it!"

"Don't be ridiculous. I'm going to my room now. I want to be *alone!*"

"Not yet. Listen to me. Did you hear what that policeman said?"

"Yes. I wish I didn't, but I did. The next time we're in trouble I'm going to jail!"

"Not that! The policeman said he's been here before! There was some bizarre accident here twenty years ago! A *freak* accident, he said!"

"So?"

"So Mr. Wooley did something really creepy twenty years ago, and he's been holed up here ever since!"

I shook my head. "Roger, you read too many comics! Besides, you ruined my protest! I really hate you!"

Roger grinned. "No you don't. You're crazy about

me! The way you went after Dutton to protect me! I could almost like you, Laney."

"You're making things up again. Go away."

Chapter 9

[November 21 — Sunday]

This is Petrie's article that was in the paper today.

OUTRAGED CHILDREN PROTEST LOSS OF THEIR HOME

By E. Petrie
REPORTER

Police converged on 54 Hogart Street when a protest organized by a group of children apparently degenerated into a fight early yesterday morning. The children were protesting an eviction from their apartments by Edwin Archibald Dutton, the owner's agent. The three-storey house is slated to be converted into condomini- CONTINUES ON A82

81

ums. All tenants have been given notice to find other accommodation. They include the three children, their widowed mother and two senior citizens.

Victoria Applebaum, aged 72, says she will have difficulty relocating in time. "I have lived here for fifteen years. It will break one's heart to leave this house."

Mrs. Anne Hadley, widowed for five years, commented, "Mr. Dutton spoke of us living here for years. I was very shocked to learn we were being evicted." Mrs. Hadley was forced to sell their original home after she was laid off from her job. Their search for a new home has taken the Hadleys to three locations in the last year.

Roger Hadley, nine, said, "Dutton is ruining my life!" Emma Hadley, five, said she won't leave "because this is home, and the other places never were."

Elaine Hadley, twelve, explained that she organized the protest to call attention to their plight. "If people knew what Mr. Dutton is doing to us, they wouldn't let him."

The other tenant, Edwin Wooley, declined to be interviewed.

The owner could not be reached for comment.

"This is another example of how inner-city development affects lower-income city residents," Councilwoman Ellen Petrov said. Planning officials admit there will soon be a very limited number of low-priced apartments available in the city's core. The high cost of real estate is blamed.

Police were called to the scene of the otherwise peaceful demonstration when Roger Hadley and Dutton apparently came to blows. Roger was bruised in the incident. Elaine Hadley and Emma Hadley and Victoria Applebaum were allegedly involved as well. No charges were laid.

Neighbours insist the Hadleys are not troublemakers. Mrs. Delores Bauer of 57 Hogart Street said, "I think it's a crime to throw them out into the street." Anastasia Newman, ten, of 53 Hogart Street commented, "Aren't those kids great?"

There was a picture of Dutton, Roger, Emma and me in a tangle. Officer Warren and the policewoman were trying to untangle us. Mr. Dutton's face looked like he was going to explode. Miss Applebaum was next to us, looking mad.

Mom didn't seem to appreciate all the coverage we got. "How did this Petrie person find out about the job I lost, and our house? I didn't tell her," she said.

"I did," Roger said proudly.

"I should have known." Mom sighed.

Roger strutted around the kitchen, waving the article under everyone's nose. "Don't I look good? See? That's me!"

"Winson looks good too," Emma said.

"I hope I don't get fired," Mom said, chewing her lip.

"Why would they fire you?" I asked.

"Sleepwell's a very conservative company. If someone there reads this article they might think I'm a troublemaker."

"But they can't fire you for what a reporter says," I told her. "You haven't done anything wrong. What matters is the paper has shown what a horrible man Dutton is. Isn't that right? No one will invest in the house now, and we won't have to move."

"This is so great," Roger crowed. "We won, we won!"

Mom shook her head. "That doesn't necessarily follow," she said. "Don't get your hopes up."

"But Mom! What about the power of the press?"

"Elaine, don't encourage your brother. We have to

be realistic. Dutton might not be bothered by bad publicity."

"He'll come here and apologize," Roger insisted. "Just see if I'm not right. Hey! There's someone at the door. That might be him now, ready to eat a word sandwich."

It was Delores Bauer. She had a huge casserole in her hands. "I think it's terrible, what Dutton's doing to you folks. How can I help?"

"Why, thank you," Mom said. "Um, would you like a cup of coffee?"

Three more neighbours brought over casseroles, enough salad for an army, and an enormous jar of cinnamon-spiced crab apples. "They're my specialty!" old Mrs. Rodale confided.

"This is so kind of you," Mom said, over and over.

After they left she said, "I never knew what nice neighbours we had here. I wish we didn't have to leave, when we're just getting to know them."

The phone started to ring then. A bunch of people called to give advice. They thought we should barricade the street, or chain ourselves to the front door, or move to Mexico. There were a couple of other calls, but Mom wouldn't tell us the other suggestions. Her face was red when she put the phone down, though.

"Wow!" Roger said. "We're famous!"

"I don't want to be famous," Mom snapped. She unplugged the phone.

Mrs. Gertrude Clooney appeared at our door with

a big chocolate cake and a little girl named Clara. "We live at number 64. My daughter is the same age as your Emma, so I thought maybe — Do you think they might like to play together?" She frowned. "You can never tell with children." She watched intently as Clara and Emma eyed each other.

Emma was the first to speak. "I hate raisins," she said.

"I um — like them," Clara said.

"I hate pink dresses," Emma said.

Clara looked down at the one she was wearing. It was pink.

I figured Emma had just blown her chance to have a *real* friend.

But Clara didn't seem to mind. "My mom makes me wear them," she said. "She thinks they look cute!"

Emma nodded. *"My* mom makes me wear hats even when it's not cold out."

Clara nodded too, then she and Emma went off together.

"Oh," said Mrs. Clooney. "My, my."

Roger plugged the phone back in when Mom wasn't looking. Someone from a newspaper named *Tales of Tragedy* wanted to tell our story.

"We are not a tragedy!" Mom snapped into the receiver. She unplugged the phone again and warned Roger not to touch it.

Dutton didn't come to apologize. He slipped a note under our door at nine o'clock:

*This is to inform you that I will be
showing potential investors
through the house this week. Any
attempt at interference will be met
by legal action.*
                    E. A. Dutton.

"I don't believe it," Roger said.

"It didn't work, did it?" I asked Mom.

"I'm afraid not. You did your best, but we're still
going to have to move."

LANEY'S LAW NUMBER 45:
The power of the press isn't worth spit!

Emma climbed up her dresser onto the top of the old
wooden frame over her window curtains. Mom got
her down and moved her dresser away from the
window. After that Emma stole all Roger's comics
and hid them under her bed.

"Winson did it! Winson's really mad!" Emma
claimed when Roger found them.

"Emma, I'm going to deck you!" he said. "Mom,
lock Emma in her closet or something!"

"No one is getting locked in her closet, and no one
is going to be decked. We are a family and we're going
to act like one! Emma, we need to have a talk. Wait
for me in your room. Roger, we have to make allow-
ances for Emma because she's the youngest. She's
upset about moving."

"So am I!"

"I know, Roger. We all are."

I read the article four times while Mom put Emma and Roger to bed. Then I went to find her. She was sitting at the kitchen table, circling ads for apartments in red pencil.

"What's an agent, Mom?"

"Someone who acts on another person's behalf. Why?"

"Well it says here Dutton is the owner's agent. I thought Dutton *owned* the house."

"Oh. Hmm . . . " Mom said. "So did I."

"But he's the landlord."

"Sometimes the landlord and the owner of a building can be two different people."

"Oh." I frowned. "Then it says, 'The owner could not be reached for comment.' Does that mean the owner wouldn't talk to Petrie?"

"Maybe. Or Petrie couldn't find him."

"So . . . that means Dutton doesn't actually own the house. Someone else does. Right?"

"I suppose so. It doesn't really matter, though. We're being evicted just the same."

"Unless Dutton gives in."

"Yes."

"But it would really be the owner giving in. I mean, *Dutton* told us about being evicted, but the *owner* decided to turn the house into condominiums. Is that what it means?"

"I guess it does, Laney. But I wish you'd stop worrying about this." Mom put her arm around me. "You tried to change things. You accomplished a lot — not in exactly the way I would have chosen, but you did. Now it's time to get on with our lives, and stop trying to change things that can't be changed. I'm sorry."

"I'm sorry, too, Mom. About, you know, well . . . everything."

She hugged me. "I know. Me too. Getting angry at each other doesn't help much, does it? We'll get through this. I promise."

"Okay."

"Now off to bed with you, and sleep tight."

I went to my room, then went back to ask Mom something else. "A councillor got quoted, and planning officials said something. *They* could be reached. Why couldn't Petrie reach the owner?"

"Councillors and planning officials hold public office. They have to talk to reporters. Private people don't have to."

"Oh. Good night, Mom."

"Good night, Laney. We'll start packing tomorrow."

LANEY'S LAW NUMBER 46:
Maybe I can't change the world after all.

Chapter 10

This morning Mom found six bags of groceries on the front porch, addressed to her, and a jar of pennies. One bag was full of whole-wheat bread, canned beans, canned ham, canned peas and canned carrots.

"I hate canned stuff," Roger said.

Another bag held three jars of anchovies.

"Yuck!" Roger said.

The other bags contained apples, oranges, broccoli and tinned tuna. Mom did not celebrate. She phoned the Salvation Army and arranged to have the donated food and money picked up.

"Can't we keep the pennies?" Roger asked.

"No," Mom said. "This city is full of people who really need help. These things should go to them. Come straight home from school today and don't talk to strangers."

Mom was not calm when we got home from school. At work someone had left an envelope of money on her desk. No one would admit to putting it there, so she stuck it in the coffee fund jar when no one was looking. Two of her co-workers spent the lunch hour saying how sorry they felt for us, and her boss asked if there would be any more trouble. Mom told them no.

When she came home there was a letter in our post-box offering to set up a donations account at a local bank, so people could collect money to help us.

"We don't need anyone's charity!" she said. "We've always made it on our own, and we're going to keep doing that! You are not to accept money or food from anyone!"

LANEY'S LAW NUMBER 47:
Being famous isn't like what you think.

Miss Applebaum brought a tray of cookies upstairs at dinner time. "Please don't make us give them back," Roger said. Just in case, he grabbed a handful.

"Are you getting strange phone calls?" Mom asked her.

"Yes. One is highly amused at their content. One gentleman called and suggested I might want to marry him! He seemed to think this was the perfect solution. I declined."

We laughed.

Roger guffawed. "Someone wanted to marry you?" He laughed so hard he dropped three cookies.

"One was amused, yes. But not quite *that* amused!" Miss Applebaum told him. Her hair was auburn today. "It is quite heart-warming to see how many people wish to lend us their support, is it not?"

"Er, I suppose so," Mom said.

"I am so glad we met. I barely knew you before. And now I feel quite . . . " Miss Applebaum ran out of words.

"I'm glad we got to know you, too," Mom said warmly. "Why don't you stay for dinner. We're still working on the lasagna Mrs. Bauer brought. There's plenty. Do you like lasagna?"

"I like everything," Miss Applebaum said, "but especially I like meals someone else has cooked!" She looked at Roger as he wolfed down the cookies. "Such charming children! One almost regrets not having any of one's own."

[November 23 — Tuesday]

Roger didn't meet me at the front door of the school, like he usually does Tuesdays, when our classes finish at the same time. I found him sitting in his classroom, slumped over a book.

"What happened?" I asked.

Miss Hutchinson looked up from her desk at the

front of the room and answered me. "Roger has been given a detention for fighting in the schoolyard."

Roger glowered at his teacher. "Speedo Morgan said we were orphans and we were poor as dirt! I *had* to make him take it back. It wasn't my fault."

"Using your fists is not an acceptable way to solve an argument," she said. "I'm keeping you here so you will remember that."

"You're not keeping Speedo Morgan!"

"His mother took him home. He has a black eye."

Roger managed to frown and grin at the same time.

"I'll see you later," I said.

Petrie was glad to see me when I arrived at the offices of the *Daily News*. At least that's what she said.

"Why, it's the famous protester of Hogart Street! Glad to see you, kid."

"Way to go, Ellen!" Mai-Lin said, grinning. She gave me a thumbs-up sign. Her nail polish was black today.

"Elaine," I said.

"Whatever. We're all proud of you here."

"You are?"

"All newshounds love a political activist!"

"A what?"

Petrie steered me away from Mai-Lin's desk. "What can I do for you, Elaine? Sorry I had to rush off Saturday, but I had a deadline to meet. You understand."

"That's okay. And I'm sorry Roger ruined my protest."

"Believe me, he didn't."

"But he made Dutton call the police!"

Petrie leaned toward me. "If the police hadn't come, the editor probably wouldn't have printed the story. I liked it enough, but he wouldn't have. The picture of the police trying to peel you and your brother and sister off Dutton clinched it!"

"So Roger got us in the newspaper?"

"In a way, yes. Did it work? Any sign of the eviction being called off?"

I shook my head.

"I'm sorry to hear it. Really." She shrugged. "It was worth a try, kid. I hope you find a good new place for yourselves."

"Thanks," I said.

"Well, I've got another story to write, so unless you have another hot lead . . . "

"Do you mind if I ask you something?"

"Sure, but make it fast. I've got to go over to the city clerk's office."

"The what?"

"The city clerk's office at City Hall. Records are kept there. What's your question?"

"Do you know who owns our house?"

"No. Information like that is kept at City Hall by the clerk. The clerk's office is closed on the weekend, so I couldn't look it up, and Dutton wouldn't tell. Our editor wanted the story in the Sunday edition — a hearts-and-flowers sort of story, so I never did look it up."

"What do you mean about looking it up? You mean if Dutton won't tell, there's another way to find out? How?"

"That's pretty simple. Records are kept of who owns what, and anyone can go and find out."

"Anyone can go? Even a twelve-year-old?"

Petrie grinned. "Yes, but you would have to know how to do it. City officials are not noted for their helpfulness."

"Oh," I said.

"Luckily, I know how," Petrie said. "I'm going there anyway. I'll show you."

"You will?"

Petrie smiled. "If you ever go into politics, remind me not to run against you."

"Why?"

"That's the beauty of it. You don't even know how good you are!"

"I am? At what?"

"At getting what you want, Elaine Hadley. Does your mother know where you are? Phone her, and get permission for this little foray." Petrie held up her hand. "I promise solemnly to drop you off at home after we hit the records office. I wouldn't abandon a piranha in that place!"

Petrie talked non-stop while we drove to the city clerk's office, about how hard she had studied to become a reporter, and how she worked at a small local newspaper for years before coming to work at the *Daily News*.

"You don't look that old," I told her.

She grinned. "What a smooth talker!"

"Do you have another name?"

"Do I! I have three other names. Eleanor Agatha Geraldine Petrie!"

"Wow!"

"Exactly! That's why I go by Petrie."

"I see."

"I thought you would."

At the clerk's office Petrie asked for access to some files and looked through them until she found our address. She showed me the line, whistled and said, "Well, what do you know?"

Two city officials asked her to be quiet. I don't even know how to whistle, but if I did I would have whistled then too, no matter who told me to be quiet.

After the visit to City Hall, Petrie dropped me at home. "Say, maybe I'll try to sell the editor on doing a follow-up story on your family. Would you mind?"

"I wouldn't, but my mom might. There have been some pretty strange phone calls."

Petrie nodded. "Sorry about that — the down side of fame. Don't worry, kid. It will be over soon. Fame doesn't last long. Maybe I'll drop by before moving day and see how you are, story or no story."

"I'd like that."

Roger was waiting for me on the front porch when I got there.

"I was right! I was right!" he crowed. "You should

pay me a zillion dollars, Laney! I'm great!"

"Why?"

"Because Mr. Wooley *does* have a secret!"

"I know," I said. "But how do *you* know?"

"I called that big policeman and he told me."

"But how did *he* know? Wait a minute. What did he tell you?"

We both said our secrets at the same time. They weren't exactly the same.

"Wow!" I said. "I didn't know that!"

"Wow!" Roger echoed, doing a high-five. "*Two* secrets! And in just one day! Bet you Mr. Wooley has aliens too."

We hurried inside and knocked on Miss Applebaum's door.

"The redoubtable Elaine! The ferocious Roger! How delightful to see you both. Is something wrong?"

I started to tell her what I'd found out. Roger kept interrupting, trying to get his story in before mine. But somehow she got most of the facts.

"I don't believe it!" she gasped.

"Yeah? Well you'd better believe it!" Roger said. "And *I* found out!" He was still grinning.

"We thought we'd better talk to Mr. Wooley," I suggested.

"Yeah!" Roger said.

Miss Applebaum nodded. Her eyes flashed. "But this changes everything! One is simply astonished! I must phone Thornton at once! His services will be needed."

Chapter 11

"This is amazing!" Mom said when we told her.

"Winson doesn't understand. So we don't have to move?" Emma asked.

"I'm not sure, Emma."

"Winson and me won't move anyway," Emma said.

"So you've said." Mom sighed.

"We're going to see Mr. Wooley now," I said.

"I want to tell Mom," Roger interrupted. "We're going to tell Mr. Wooley to his face! Maybe after that we'll deck him."

"Roger! I warned you about that kind of talk! If

you can't control yourself you can't go."

"But Mom! I'm the detective. I found out. Laney is my assistant."

"No threats and no fighting!" Mom warned. "I'd better go with you this time to make sure."

"You never let me have any fun!"

"Roger — "

"Okay, okay. But be prepared for aliens!"

We trooped down the stairs.

Miss Applebaum and Thornton met us outside Mr. Wooley's door. "One is almost too perturbed to speak," Miss Applebaum said. "Thornton will demand an explanation."

"I will represent your interests," Thornton said. "Demanding isn't always the right approach." He had on a dark grey suit. He looked about ten years older than before, more like a lawyer, but he sounded exactly the same. He looked us over. "It might be better if I went alone."

Miss Applebaum drew herself up to her full height. "One must come. You cannot fail to see this! Who is paying you?"

"No one is paying me," Thornton said.

"Oh . . . Yes . . . But the principle is the same, is it not?"

"If you really have to come, come. But remember, insults are not likely to lead to an agreement."

"Quite!" Miss Applebaum dimmed her eyes a fraction. "One takes your meaning."

Mr. Wooley opened the door at the sound of my voice.

"May we speak with you, Mr. Wooley?" Thornton said. When Mr. Wooley saw Thornton he tried to close the door. Miss Applebaum shoved her foot into the crack, preventing him. Mr. Wooley blinked rapidly and stared at the floor.

"We want to talk to you, Mr. Wooley," I said. "Can we come in?"

Mr. Wooley started to shake his head.

"Winson wants to come in!" Emma said. "Do you have any more umbrellas?"

Mr. Wooley blinked. He looked at Emma. Then he stepped back and opened the door.

His sweater wasn't buttoned at all today. Rice Krispies were stuck to the front of his shirt. His socks had drooped down over his slippers as if life was too much for them. They were the colour of mud — grey mud on one foot and black mud on the other.

"Thank you for seeing us," Thornton said.

"I am so . . . I cannot . . . What can I . . . ?" He couldn't meet our eyes.

For the first time we saw Mr. Wooley's apartment.

"At last!" Roger cried, and then stopped dead. "No aliens," he said. "No cats."

"P–pardon?" Mr. Wooley asked.

The apartment was not full of pickled cats. It was not full of aliens. It was full of umbrellas. Crammed into every corner, spilled out over the floor, stacked on chairs and tables and mantlepiece, were umbrellas of every size and shape. TRULY STRANGE OLD MAN LIVES WITH A ZILLION UMBRELLAS.

"My word," Miss Applebaum said. "You are certainly prepared for rain!"

There were paper umbrellas with an oriental look, and plain black umbrellas. There were huge umbrellas in rainbow colours and tiny parasols with fringes. Some umbrella handles looked like duck heads or snakes. One spectacular umbrella, open in the middle of the room, was painted with red dragons, their wings spread in flight. Emma walked up to it and stared.

Mr. Wooley took it up, ducked his head and twirled it. "You s—see. When you do this they seem to fly."

"Oh!" Emma said. She smiled. "Winson likes it."

Mr. Wooley blushed. "I like it too." Then he looked up. "This is . . . my Collection."

"How many do you have?" Mom asked, looking amazed.

"One hundred and twenty-two." He took umbrellas off the threadbare sofa and chairs, so we could sit. He put them down very gently.

"There's a matter we wish to discuss with you," Thornton said.

Roger looked behind the furniture hopefully. "No cages," he muttered. "No jars."

I took a deep breath. "*You* own this house, Mr. Wooley," I said.

Mr. Wooley lowered his eyes and nodded.

"But you said you didn't want to move," I said.

"Yeah!" Roger said loudly. "So why are you? Does

it have anything to do with aliens?"

"Wh–what?"

Thornton put up a hand. "We would like to know, if you don't mind . . . Why are you selling the house, Mr. Wooley?" he asked.

Mr. Wooley couldn't seem to speak. He limped over to a desk, reached under an umbrella and handed Thornton a well-worn legal paper. Thornton scanned it quickly.

"Mr. Wooley, I wish you had consulted someone before you signed this agreement. The terms of this contract are so — Well, I have never seen another like it!"

"What is it?" Mom asked.

Thornton looked up. "Perhaps you'd like to explain, Mr. Wooley."

Mr. Wooley shook his head and gestured to Thornton.

"You borrowed money from Mr. Dutton twenty years ago at a very high interest rate. Isn't that so?" Thornton said gently.

Mr. Wooley nodded. He looked at the floor. "It was necessary to . . . to make the apartments."

"I see." Thornton nodded.

"I, I couldn't afford to live in the house alone . . . "

Thornton frowned. "But you must have been employed."

"I was, and then — "

"I bet that's when you had your freaky accident!" Roger said. He swaggered. "I phoned that policeman.

A long time ago Mr. Wooley had this accident, see, and he was hurt real bad. And the police came then — and that policeman, Officer Warren, he's my friend, so he looked it up for me — he said I could probably find the story in the old newspapers, but I told him I couldn't wait."

"Roger, please," Mom said. "Let Mr. Wooley speak."

Roger scowled.

Now I saw that Mr. Wooley leaned on a cane almost all the time.

"Yes, I had an accident . . . I lost my job at the umbrella factory after that. S–so I borrowed money from Mr. Dutton to renovate the house and divide it into apartments. New plumbing was needed, and, and roofing." Mr. Wooley's voice failed.

"That cost a great deal of money, I expect," Thornton said. "You probably expected the rent your tenants paid to cover your loan payments, your living expenses and the upkeep of the house."

Mr. Wooley nodded. "But . . . it didn't." He couldn't seem to go on.

Thornton took up the story. "So you couldn't manage the payments after all."

"I fell behind."

"And you were paying Dutton a very high salary to act as landlord."

"I, I couldn't manage things alone."

"I see."

"I am very sorry to hear about your misfortune,

Mr. Wooley," Mom said. Mr. Wooley nodded miserably.

Thornton looked at us. "There is a clause in this contract that gives Mr. Dutton the right to evict the tenants, including Mr. Wooley himself, and sell the house if Mr. Wooley has not cleared the debt by . . . Just one moment." Thornton flipped through the contract. It was many pages long. "By this coming Friday!"

"What? That dreadful man is even worse than we thought!" Miss Applebaum cried. "He has taken advantage of your difficulties. He is altogether detestable!"

Thornton frowned. "He has the legal right."

Miss Applebaum looked like a volcano about to erupt. "That is not the point. What he has done is absolutely wrong, and the law was never meant to protect wrongdoers."

Mr. Wooley glanced up. He blinked at Miss Applebaum. "I, I'm sorry. You all have to move now, because . . . of me."

Thornton read the papers. "But you still have three days, Mr. Wooley. Mr. Dutton has already begun showing the house to investors. He has no right to do that!"

"He . . . he knows I cannot pay."

"I suppose, strictly speaking, he would be within the law as long as no contracts are signed before midnight, Friday night."

"There must be a way to break this abominable

agreement," Miss Applebaum said, her lips a thin line. "Thornton, please!"

"Let me read it again," Thornton said. A battered card table stood in the middle of the living room. Thornton carefully lifted umbrellas off it, sat down and took out a notebook. He pored over the document. He jotted down points. He seemed to forget there was anyone else in the room.

"Mr. Wooley, would you kindly allow one to prepare a pot of tea?" Miss Applebaum asked.

Mr. Wooley nodded. He sank down onto the couch, his hands trembling. Emma was still sitting in the middle of the room, twirling the dragon umbrella.

Miss Applebaum returned from the kitchen with an old chipped teapot and some mismatched cups and saucers. She put them on an old side-table. "Anne, pour!" she commanded my mother.

Mom poured the tea and handed the cups around. We sat and sipped the tea in uncomfortable silence while Thornton shuffled pages. Miss Applebaum went down to her own apartment and returned with a plate of buttered scones and a pot of homemade jam. "Mr. Wooley, one requires more than a dry crust of bread for life. One requires taste, variety. Your kitchen is inadequately stocked. I shall personally see to its improvement."

"I, I don't have the money," Mr. Wooley said.

"My nephew will see to that. It is past time for you to be rid of that detestable thorn in your side — that Dutton!"

Mr. Wooley blinked rapidly. As soon as Miss Applebaum caught his eye, he returned to staring at the floor.

We ate Miss Applebaum's scones while Thornton worked. The scones were very good. At last Thornton put down the papers and looked up. His face was grim.

"This contract was written by a diabolical genius. The only way to save this house is to pay off Mr. Wooley's debt *before* midnight Friday night."

Mr. Wooley wilted.

"How much money do you owe, Mr. Wooley? If I might ask," Thornton said.

"It doesn't matter how much money you owe Mr. Dutton," Miss Applebaum said fiercely. "We will pool our resources together and pay off the debt! We will defeat that despicable man at his own game!"

Mr. Wooley fumbled in his pocket. He took out a worn little notebook. He handed it to Thornton. "I still owe twenty-seven thousand, one hundred and seventeen dollars and thirty-four cents."

"Oh!" Miss Applebaum's face fell. "Oh!" She sank down onto the couch beside Mr. Wooley. "That is a great deal of money."

Chapter 12

[Still November 23 — Tuesday]

"Winson doesn't understand," Emma said. "Why is everyone so sad?"

"Mr. Wooley owes Mr. Dutton a lot of money. Mr. Dutton is making us all move out of the house."

"We should deck Dutton!" Roger said.

Mom gave him a look.

"Well we should!"

"Winson thinks so too!" Emma said.

"Emma, please!" Mom sighed. "That *is* a lot of money."

"One doesn't see how we could raise that amount," Miss Applebaum said. Her shoulders drooped. "Did you say twenty-seven thousand dollars?"

Thornton frowned. "I was hoping it would be less than that."

Mr. Wooley turned away and blew his nose. "I am so very . . . sorry. So very . . . "

"It's not your fault," I said. Mr. Wooley looked up at me, his vague blue eyes watery. I couldn't stand it. "There must be something we can do," I said, thinking out loud. "Couldn't we borrow the money from someone else?"

Miss Applebaum sat up straight. "Elaine is right. We must think!" She turned to her nephew. "Am I to understand, Thornton, that the terms of this loan are less equitable than the terms a bank might offer?"

Thornton nodded. "Considerably."

"Then why not negotiate a new loan with a bank, so Mr. Wooley could pay off that dreadful man and be rid of him?"

"Because bank loans take time. I could probably obtain a favourable loan for Mr. Wooley, but papers must be drawn up, inspectors must look over the house, officials must be consulted. If I had just a little more time I could do it. In three days, no."

"That is unfortunate."

There was a pause.

"We can't give up now," I said. "I have thirteen dollars and twenty-seven cents I saved for Christmas. Mr. Wooley can have it. I could earn some more money raking leaves. I know I could. Mr. Wooley can have that too."

"But I couldn't take it," Mr. Wooley said, his voice shaking.

"I'll loan it to you then. You can pay it back whenever you have enough money. I don't care how long I wait." Everyone looked at me. "Well, if you have no money, isn't thirteen dollars better than nothing?"

"Indeed it is," Miss Applebaum said softly. I had never heard her speak softly before.

"I'm proud of you, Laney," Mom said. Her voice was soft too. "But it isn't enough money to change things," she added.

"It is, however, a start," Miss Applebaum said, "and an inspiration. We shouldn't give up yet." Her eyes caught fire. "I shall follow your lead, Laney. One has put aside a little money in case of emergency. I can offer two thousand four hundred dollars." Miss Applebaum's gaze fell on her nephew.

Thornton winced and cleared his throat. "Stop looking at me like that, Aunt Victoria. Oh, very well. Mr. Wooley, I can lend you eight thousand, nine hundred dollars." He shrugged his shoulders. "I've been saving for a car, but it can wait."

Miss Applebaum smiled at him. "You have always been my favourite nephew. I see now I was not mistaken in my judgement."

"I'm your only nephew."

"Even so." She paused. "Would the bank lend *you* money?"

"No. I haven't finished paying off my student loans yet."

"Ah."

Thornton got his chequebook out and began to write. Mr. Wooley had been looking stunned, but now he spoke. "But you mustn't! It's so much money — "

"One will insist as much as is necessary," Miss Applebaum said.

"B–but — "

"Savings are only pieces of paper," Miss Applebaum said. "A car is only a metal box. This house is our *home!* We must save it!"

"Do you really think there is a chance?" Mom asked.

"Elaine seems to think so," Miss Applebaum said. "I am beginning to have confidence in her judgment. Thornton, you *are* keeping track of these figures?"

Thornton grabbed his notebook and nodded.

Mr. Wooley was beyond words.

"I have five dollars and thirty-five cents," Roger said, "but I have to get it back later."

Mr. Wooley nodded, dazed. Mom smiled at Roger and turned to the others. "I'm afraid my bank balance is quite low."

"One understands," Miss Applebaum said.

"But we're getting there, aren't we?" I said.

Both Thornton and Miss Applebaum nodded. "May I use your telephone, Mr. Wooley?" Miss Applebaum asked.

Mr. Wooley nodded. "H–how can I ever thank you — "

"You don't have to, Mr. Wooley," I said.

He looked at me. For the first time he smiled — a small, shy movement at the corners of his mouth.

Miss Applebaum spoke on the telephone. I was glad she wasn't talking to me. When she put down the phone she smiled. "Thornton, your mother has seen the wisdom of lending us a further five thousand dollars. She can go on a cruise some other time."

Emma got up from the floor, reached into her pocket and put a purple dime in Mr. Wooley's hands. "Do you mind jam?" she asked.

"No," Mr. Wooley said. He showed Emma another umbrella while Miss Applebaum and Thornton bent over the figures.

"Your umbrellas are magic," Emma told Mr. Wooley.

Mr. Wooley smiled shakily. "I think so too." He opened one that showed a whole circus. As he twirled it circus bells rang. "They are set into the handle, you see . . . "

Roger picked up an umbrella with a snake's-head handle. "Neat!"

"Ask before touching someone else's things, Roger," Mom said.

"Oh, yeah. Can I open this one?"

Mr. Wooley nodded. The snake umbrella shimmered with sleek painted scales.

"Wow!" Roger said.

"You can keep my ten cents," Emma said.

"Thank you." Mr. Wooley handed the dime to Thornton.

"Anne, my dear, your children — they're simply astonishing!" said Miss Applebaum.

"Yes," Mom said. "They are."

"Do we have enough money yet?" I asked Thornton.

"We have sixteen thousand three hundred and eighteen dollars and seventy-two cents."

I bit my lip.

"But where are we to get the rest of the money?" Miss Applebaum asked.

No one said anything.

"We're going to have to move after all," Roger said in disgust.

I thought we'd done it. I really did. There didn't seem to be anything left to say.

"To lose to that horrible man now, after all our efforts!" Miss Applebaum said. "One is quite infuriated!"

Mr. Wooley's shoulders slumped. "Th–thank you anyway. I will never forget — "

Mom looked at him. "If we can meet friends like you where we move, perhaps it isn't so bad."

Emma stood up. "Mr. Wooley and me aren't moving, ever," she said. *"This* is home!"

Mr. Wooley stared at her.

"Perhaps the children and I had better go home now," Mom said. "It was very nice meeting you and your wonderful umbrellas, Mr. Wooley. We're not blaming you."

"Didn't you hear me?" Emma said, as we went up the stairs.

"We heard you, Muffin," Mom said. She put an arm around Emma and drew her close. Emma sniffed.

LANEY'S LAW NUMBER 48:
Life stinks!

Chapter 13

Mom spent a long time settling Emma in bed. Emma got up three times and came out to wander the apartment before she finally went to sleep. Mom talked to Roger and me after that.

"No one could have better children. Don't look so sad," she said. "We'll find ways to visit our friends after we move. I promise."

I couldn't sleep that night. I heard someone moving around the apartment after I went to bed, but figured I should leave Mom alone for awhile.

I was almost asleep when I heard Roger yell, "You tore some of my comics, you rat! I'll deck you, Emma!"

Then he said, "Emma? *Emma? Mo-om, Emma's gone!*"

Mom and I got to Emma's room at the same time. We searched under the bed, in the closet, on top of the closet shelf, on top of every piece of furniture.

"Emma, come out!" Mom cried. "This isn't funny!"

Then we searched the rest of the apartment. All the time Mom's voice got louder and louder.

"Emma! I don't care what you've done. Just come out now, Muffin!"

Then the phone rang. I heard Mom say, "What! Oh my god! You must be wrong, Mr. Trumpkin!"

Mom's feet pounded down the hallway. A window crashed open. "Oh no!" Mom moaned.

I sprinted into the hall to see Mom staring out of the living room window, her face white. From somewhere outside came a small piping voice.

"Oh, no! We won't go!"

Mom ran back to the phone. Her voice was ragged. "Call 9-1-1, Mr. Trumpkin!" she cried. "No. Hang up and I'll call them myself."

"Mom, what is it?" I asked.

"Emma's on the roof!"

"What!" Roger's eyes popped open.

"How did she get there?" Mom asked in a strained voice. "I was sure she was asleep. Hello? This is an emergency! My five-year-old daughter is on the roof. The house is three stories tall! We're at 54 Hogart Street. Hurry, please hurry!"

A heap of cardboard boxes lay on the living room

floor. They hadn't been there when we went to bed.

"She couldn't have climbed out her window. There's nothing to hang onto there! A rope! I need a rope!"

I ran to my closet and got Roger's bed-sheet rope. Mom took it without a word. She tested all the knots, leaned out the window and shouted. "Hang on, Emma. Mommy's coming!" She tied the rope around her waist and then around the couch. She shoved the heavy couch over to the window as if it weighed nothing, and climbed onto the window ledge.

"Mom, how will you hang on?"

"I don't know. Oh, how did Emma get up there?"

"Don't go out there, Mom!" Roger cried.

"I have to, Roger."

Roger stuck his head out the window. "Emma, I don't care about the comics. You can come down. I won't deck you! I promise!"

"Elaine, run downstairs," Mom cried. "Find out if Mr. Wooley or Miss Applebaum have a ladder."

"Mom!" I said. "Be careful!"

"I'll hold the couch!" Roger said.

"All right. Go, Laney. *Now!* How can it take so long for the trucks to come?"

I pounded on Mr. Wooley's door first. "Mr. Wooley! We need your help! Emma's on the roof! Have you got a ladder?"

I didn't wait for the door to open. I couldn't. My feet took me to Miss Applebaum's door before I realized I'd moved.

"Miss Applebaum!" Her door sprang open. Her eyes and hair were wild. "Emma's on the roof! Have you got a ladder?"

A chartreuse robe billowed around her. She gripped my shoulder. "We'll get her down, Laney! One has no ladder but there must be such a contraption somewhere. I'll search the basement. You start knocking on the neighbours' doors."

I burst out the front door, tripped on the porch stairs and skidded onto the lawn, headfirst. I rolled to my feet and sped to the next house.

Overhead Emma chanted, "Oh no! We won't go!"

I looked up. Sitting on the pitched roof beneath a full moon was Emma in her yellow coat. She was yelling. Then she started waving her fist. Suddenly she lurched to the side and stopped yelling. She started to slide. I heard her scream, "Help!"

"Emma!" Below her, Mom inched her way up the stone wall, hanging onto an old vine. She was still a long way from the roof. "Emma, hang on!" Mom called.

Far below Mr. Trumpkin was climbing a ladder. But the ladder wasn't long enough. I saw he wouldn't make it. "Mrs. Hadley, it's too dangerous," he called, but Mom didn't turn back.

Lights flicked on as I pounded on the door of the next house. The door flew open. A man in pyjamas stared at me. "My sister's on the roof," I said. "Do you have a ladder?"

He looked up. "Have you called for help?"

"Yes, but they haven't come yet."

Very faintly now I heard sirens.

"I'll find a ladder. I think the Bauers have a longer one. Eleanor, call the Bauers! You go home now, kid. Help is on the way."

I ran back to the porch.

"Mo-om!" Emma screamed overhead.

Mom was halfway to the roof. She had run out of vine. She scrambled for a hold higher up, but I saw she couldn't find one. My legs froze. Mom looked down. "Elaine, get in the house."

I ran up the stairs. A shambling figure appeared before me at the second floor. I didn't recognize it at first. Then I saw it was Mr. Wooley in an old bathrobe.

"My sister's on the roof," I said. "We don't know how she got there."

Mr. Wooley's face turned white. "I do."

"What?"

"At least, I–I might know — "

"What? What do you know?"

"Th–there's a trapdoor," he said shakily. "In the living room ceiling."

"No there isn't. I live there and I've never seen it."

"It's hidden," Mr. Wooley said. "You'd never see it unless you knew. I don't understand how — "

"Where is it?" I cried.

"A–above the mantelpiece. But how could she — ?"

"Emma climbs. Never mind that. Tell me quickly. How does it open?"

"Th—there's a trick switch. Turn the fifth plaster rose from the left. I'll come." He leaned on his cane and shuffled out his apartment door.

Before Mr. Wooley had reached the stairs, I was up them. A shaking Roger helped me drag the heavy chair over to the mantelpiece. We kicked the boxes out of the way. Roger didn't say a word.

I climbed quickly onto the mantelpiece and frantically counted roses. They were cracked. Some pieces had fallen off. I twisted the fifth rose. Nothing happened. I twisted harder. It broke off in my hand. I saw a stain on the wall I hadn't noticed before. An entire rose was missing — the second rose. I counted again and twisted the fourth rose. Above my head the cracks in the ceiling widened. A trapdoor creaked open. A dark hole gaped over me, but as my eyes adjusted I could see a ladder attached to the door. In seconds I was on my way up.

"You can't go up there!" Roger croaked.

"Oh yes I can."

How old is this ladder, I wondered as it groaned under my feet. The darkness overhead felt like it was swallowing me. Something cold brushed against my face. I bit my lip and struck it away. It was a chain. I pulled on it. Something moved above me. Moonlight shone into the dusty attic as another trapdoor opened, with another fixed ladder attached to it.

"Mommy!" Emma screamed.

"Hang on," Mom shouted.

I climbed the ladder to the hole. From the hole I

looked out over the roof. I was at the peak. The roof fell away steeply on both sides of me. Emma must have been sitting on the thin edge of the peak. She was flat on the steep pitch now, though, clinging to the shingles a metre away from me. I can't reach her, I thought. I'll have to let go of the ladder, and then I'll slide too. But I started to edge out anyway.

"I'm here, Emma," I called.

She turned her head. Her face was pinched with fear.

"Don't let go," I said. "I'm coming."

"Laney?" She shrieked as she started to slide again.

"Laney?" Mom called. "How did you — ? For goodness sake be careful. Don't take any chances."

"There's a trapdoor, Mom. Grab my hand, Em," I yelled, stretching out. No good. She was too far away. I looked back at the ladder for something to hold onto — anything, and found myself staring into Roger's terrified eyes.

"You'll fall," he said.

"No, I won't. I'll hook my ankles through the ladder. You hold onto my legs," I said.

He nodded.

Scraping at shingles for handholds, I edged out again. My ankles strained against the metal sides of the ladder. Roger's arms wrapped around my legs.

"Elaine!" Mom called. "I can't get to you. If you can't make it wait for me."

My chest was on the roof now, and then my

stomach. My head spun. I felt sick. Emma whimpered. Then I had her sticky hand in mine. I pulled with all my strength. Emma was a lot heavier than I remembered. Gasping, I drew her into my arms and passed her back toward Roger.

"Grab her," I told Roger.

"But I'll have to let go of you."

"I'm okay. Let go."

Emma was sobbing now. I knew I couldn't hold her for long. "You're all right now, Emma," I said. "Put your legs into the hole. Have you got her, Roger?"

His hands were off me. My ankles began to shake.

"I've got her."

I pulled my way back up the shingles. They were as rough as gravel. Finally I felt my right hand hook over the edge of the hole, then my left. I wiggled around, and my feet found the rungs of the ladder, but I couldn't seem to move them after that.

"Mom?" I called. "We got her."

"Thank goodness!"

"What about you?" I still couldn't see her.

"I'm all right, Laney. The vines are holding. Get back inside. I'll be there in a minute to help you."

Her voice didn't sound all right.

"Mom?"

I couldn't hear her reply. The sirens were loud, now. Then they stopped. I clung to the edge of the trapdoor while bright lights suddenly shone onto the roof. Huge ladders snaked out of the darkness. The firefighters had arrived.

"That's it, ma'am," I heard a man say. "Easy does it. I've got you now. You're going to be fine."

Another man appeared in front of me. "Are you hurt, miss?"

"N–no." Something seemed to be wrong with my voice. "Is my Mom okay?"

"Yes. She's safe now. She's on the ladder, and we're taking her down to the ground. Do you need help?"

"No. I can go down this way." But my legs seemed to be stuck. So the man came up, crept along the peak of the roof and looked me over.

"Take my arm now. I won't let you fall. You're nearly there." He helped me down through the trap-door and into the attic, which I didn't need, really. Roger was there, and he stared hard at me before the man helped me down the next ladder. Someone bald was just setting up another ladder next to the one I was on, and he helped me too. It was Mr. Trumpkin.

Miss Applebaum and Mr. Wooley were waiting in the living room. Emma was clinging to Mr. Wooley's leg, sobbing, "Won't go!" He was patting her back.

Miss Applebaum drew me into her arms. "You don't have to cry, my child. It's over now. Your family is safe. One is," her voice shook, "too relieved for words."

We all went down to meet Mom as she stepped off the ladder.

"Leave it to the professionals next time, ma'am."

Mom nodded. "There won't be a next time."

It was a long time before she let go of us.

Petrie showed up in all the commotion and began snapping pictures. "Do you have a spare room?" she asked me. "I might as well move in here. It would save me travel time."

By then I could almost laugh.

"Seriously, are you all right, kid?"

"Yes, I am, now."

"Good, 'cause I'm starting to get attached to you. Maybe we should have dinner or something some time."

Mom took me aside. "Elaine, that was a very brave thing you did, going up on the roof after Emma, but if you ever do something like that again . . . I'll deck you."

I did laugh then. When I stopped I noticed Roger watching me. "After all the times I've wanted to throttle you," I said, "I never thought you'd help me like that. Thanks, Roger. You might be a human being after all."

"Yeah, well. I did good, huh?"

"You did good. In a high place, too."

"Hey, who says I'm afraid of high places?"

I surprised even myself by trying to hug him.

He twisted away from me. "Hey!"

Roger climbed all over the ladder truck and talked the firefighters into letting him wear their hats. Mom had to pry him away from them so they could leave. They waved at us as they drove away.

Later we sat around the kitchen table — Miss Applebaum, Mr. Wooley, Mom, Roger and me, drinking Ovaltine. Emma was safely asleep in her room. The trapdoor had been temporarily nailed shut, and the cardboard boxes collapsed. She wouldn't be able to climb on them anymore.

"They made far too convenient a ladder to the mantlepiece!" Mom said. "Emma was playing with those roses before. I should have realized she would climb up there again, using the boxes!"

Miss Applebaum looked at her. "Anne, my dear, you had no way of knowing the trapdoor could be opened by twisting a plaster rose. You didn't even know the trapdoor existed! And Mr. Wooley had no way of knowing about Emma's prodigious talent for climbing. Emma's discovery was a complete accident. Neither of you must blame yourselves."

Mom managed a small smile. "My children have a talent for accidents!"

Miss Applebaum nodded admiringly. "And for discovering things!"

We drank our Ovaltine.

"Mr. Wooley, you fell off the roof a long time ago," Roger said, "didn't you?"

Mr. Wooley nodded. "Y–yes. A big truck lost control, jumped the curb and slammed into the house. I was working on the roof at the time. The noise startled me so much I lost my grip and fell. The injuries . . . I lost my job because I couldn't work. I,

I couldn't leave the house for a long time. Then I began to feel it wasn't safe to leave the house . . . "

"Who could blame one?" Miss Applebaum said. "After such a dreadful experience because of a truck? Infernal machines!"

"That was when you had the apartments made, and borrowed the money from Mr. Dutton?" Mom asked.

Mr. Wooley nodded. "The house needed so many changes to make the apartments. They were expensive." He blinked. "Then the longer I stayed inside, the harder it became to go out . . . "

"So there never were any aliens," Roger muttered. He sighed.

Mr. Wooley looked at him. "Aliens? No."

"Then who were you talking to inside your apartment?" Roger asked.

"Roger!" Mom said.

Mr. Wooley blushed. "My Collection."

Miss Applebaum smiled. "I often voice my thoughts aloud as I paint. It is part of the artistic temperament, which we obviously share."

Mr. Wooley blinked. "Maybe I shouldn't have stayed inside so long. Maybe that was a mistake."

"I made a mistake too," Roger said. "Like when Emma took my comics. I maybe shouldn't have said I was going to deck her."

Mom put her arm around Roger. "Maybe not. But she didn't climb on the roof because of you. She did that because she doesn't want to move."

Mr. Wooley looked at us. "I wish — "

"So do we, Mr. Wooley," Miss Applebaum said. "Thornton may come up with another idea yet."

"Will he?" Mr. Wooley said sadly. He cleared his throat. "I would do anything or sell anything to save our home. If only I had something of value!"

"But you do, Mr. Wooley," Miss Applebaum said. "Your Collection! Not that one would ever suggest — "

Mr. Wooley blinked. "They are just umbrellas. I never thought they were worth much money. Do you suppose anyone would want them?"

"You must have had them for years," Mom said. "Sometimes old things are valuable. *Are* they very old?"

Mr. Wooley nodded. "More than fifty-one years. Some were old when I got them and are over one hundred years old now. I collected them while I was working. They, they come from all over the world. I had friends abroad who sent me some because they knew of my interest. I used to make umbrellas, you see . . . I still do, once in a while."

"To think — we were both creating, separately, all these years, neither of us realizing . . . Your Collection is exquisite. Are you quite sure you could bear to part with it?" Miss Applebaum said softly.

"A home is more important than a collection." He looked at Emma and me. "Yes, I would sell them. But how?"

Miss Applebaum gripped his arm and stood up. "I shall telephone Thornton at once."

She went into the living room. We heard her voice. "Of course I know what time it is! Do not be impertinent! One requires assistance. Pay attention!"

She returned to the kitchen. "Thornton knows someone in the antiques business. He will call upon you first thing tomorrow morning, Mr. Wooley. He cautions us not to get our hopes up. The umbrellas may not be worth — " Miss Applebaum hesitated " — as much as one thinks."

[November 24 — Wednesday]

Too tired to write much. Slept in and went to school late. Roger and I went straight to Miss Applebaum's after school to hear the news. Thornton was already there.

An antiques man had come to see Mr. Wooley while we were at school. Miss Applebaum told us he made a lot of notes and hmmming noises. But he didn't say anything!

"I don't believe it!" Roger groaned.

"I'll let you know as soon as the dealer makes his offer," Thornton told us. "We'll have to wait."

"One doesn't have time to wait!" Miss Applebaum cried.

"I've given him a deadline. That's the best I can do," Thornton said.

"One appreciates your work, dear boy. It's just that — "

"I know."

Thornton kissed his aunt on the cheek and she absent-mindedly patted his head, as if he were a dog.

After he left we came back to our own apartment to wait. Roger muttered and moaned until I thought I'd scream. I couldn't help wondering how much longer it would be our apartment.

I started biting my fingernails. Even the news didn't seem interesting. Would we make it? Why didn't Thornton phone? Arrgh! I felt like *I'd* be an antique by the time he phoned!

LANEY'S LAW NUMBER 49:
Waiting is absolutely the worst thing in the world!

By bedtime I'd been to Miss Applebaum's apartment five times.

"We should hear later," she always said. "Can you wait longer?"

LANEY'S LAW NUMBER 50:
Why is it that everything really important seems to come 'later?'

Chapter 14

Thornton phoned! He phoned! Miss Applebaum rounded us up after school and we gathered in Mr. Wooley's apartment.

"Well? Well? One of us will surely expire from suspense if you do not enlighten us at once!" Miss Applebaum told Thornton.

"The dealer just telephoned. I have to work out the figures. I can tell you the umbrellas are worth a lot more money than we thought. It turns out one of them had been used by Queen Victoria a long time ago."

"Victoria? That's *your* name," Emma said to Miss Applebaum.

"Yes," Miss Applebaum said, "In fact, I was named after Queen Victoria. A lot of people my age were. She ruled Great Britain for a very long time and was famous."

I nodded. "I know. Queen Victoria was Queen Elizabeth's great-grandmother. I did a project on her last year at school. But how did you get the umbrella, Mr. Wooley?"

"A, a close friend of mine sent it to me as a gift from England many years ago. It's a plain umbrella — black, with a broken spoke and a wooden handle with the royal coat of arms carved in it. The umbrella had been thrown away, and came into the hands of the umbrella trade. It had been garbage, you see . . . I never really thought it would be worth so much. I almost didn't even bother to show it to the dealer."

"It's a good job you did," Thornton said. "You wouldn't believe how much money people will pay to own something royalty has owned."

"So that one broken umbrella is worth a lot?" I asked.

Thornton nodded. "More than all the others put together. That's one of the strange things about collectors. They sometimes care more about a thing a famous person owned than about a much more beautiful thing. But some of Mr. Wooley's other umbrellas are worth a lot of money because they're so unusual and beautiful."

"How much money?" Roger cried.

"Roger, please," Mom said. "It is enough?" she asked tensely.

"I'm almost finished my calculations." Thornton bent over his notepad. When he looked up his eyes were shining. "It's enough! We can pay off Dutton! We can save the house!"

Roger cheered, temporarily deafening everyone. Emma launched herself across the room and somehow ended up in Mr. Wooley's arms. Miss Applebaum and Mom embraced. Thornton stood there, grinning from ear to ear. He came over to me and stuck out his hand.

"Well done, Elaine Hadley," he said.

I couldn't think of anything to say back. Then Miss Applebaum was upon us.

"A handshake is hardly adequate!" she said, and threw her arms around us. She smelled like a vanilla milkshake. "What courage, what industry! One is so grateful to you both."

To Mr. Wooley she said, "As long as I live, I shall never forget your generous spirit." She kissed him gently on one cheek.

Then Mom was hugging me. "I'm so proud I could burst."

Roger came up and poked me. "We are so good!" he said.

"Quit poking me."

"Can't make me." He grinned.

"Can't you ever stop irritating me?"

He laughed and ran over to poke Emma. "No

more aunts!" he yelled. "No more creepy new schools! Yay!"

Everyone began to talk at once.

"What's next?"

"Do we have to do anything else?"

"Are we in time?"

"Yes, barely," Thornton said. "I'll take care of the rest of the details. I'll contact Mr. Dutton and set up an appointment for tomorrow."

"Can he make more trouble?"

"No. He's bound by the contract, just the way Mr. Wooley was."

"Then it's really over."

"No moving now. No moving ever!"

"We have a home," Mom said. "That is, if you will let us stay, Mr. Wooley."

Everyone stopped talking and looked at Mr. Wooley. We suddenly realized that he was our landlord.

"Please stay," he said shyly. "This is your home as well as mine, for as long as you want."

"That will be a very long time," Miss Applebaum said with a blinding smile. "But we must celebrate! A dinner, in two hours!" She looked thoughtful for a minute. "Yes, one has enough chocolate in the larder to manage."

Mom suggested we invite a friend to the celebration dinner, which was held in our apartment. Emma invited Clara, who said, "I won't have to wear pink, will I?"

Roger invited Anastasia. "But if your hair gets in my dinner you have to go home," he warned her.

I invited Petrie. I sat beside the phone for a long time before calling her. I didn't think she'd come, but she did. "There's a new section going into the Sunday paper called 'Kids' Beat,'" she said when I let her in. "Would you like to help with it?"

"Are you kidding? Sure!"

"We couldn't pay you very much."

"I'll do it for free!"

"Take the money, kid."

"Would you do me a favour?"

"Shoot."

"Would you please call me Laney instead of 'kid?'"

"Deal."

We shook hands.

The celebration dinner was great. Mr. Wooley came wearing neatly pressed grey pants and a sweater buttoned up the right way. Miss Applebaum wore a purple dress.

After dinner Mr. Wooley brought out six umbrellas. "There was enough money without selling these." He gave the circus umbrella to Emma.

"Oh good!" she said, clapping her hands. "That's my favourite!" She jumped onto the couch and kissed him. He blushed and smiled.

Roger got the snake umbrella. "Cool!" he said. "Do you have any more secrets? Maybe if I looked in all your drawers . . ."

"Roger," Mom said. "Don't be nosey."

"Isn't it enough for you that we have a real home now?" I asked him. "Can't you forget about your *Bizarre* comics for once?"

"Yeah, well," he said. "I'll find lots of other secrets, I bet." But he was quiet for a whole twenty minutes after that.

Miss Applebaum got a magenta umbrella covered with white and mauve butterflies. She turned pink. "Why, Mr. Wooley. It's glorious. One hardly knows what to say." She touched his arm and he didn't move away.

Mom got an umbrella that looked like a sunflower. "I love it!" she said.

Thornton got a black umbrella with a shiny wooden handle. "Perfect!" he said.

And I got the dragon umbrella.

"I saw the way you looked at it," Mr. Wooley said softly.

All dinner long we didn't hear about Winston, and Emma didn't yell once.

When Roger started talking again he said how wonderful 'we' detectives had been until I couldn't stand it anymore. "Stop it, or you'll be sorry!" I said.

"Can't make me!" he said. "We, we, we . . . "

I decided not to throttle him, in spite of that.

We voted on who should hand Mr. Dutton the cheque, since it was everyone's money. I won the vote.

"Quiet everyone," Miss Applebaum said, standing up. "Once in a very long time a person comes along who is not satisfied to leave things as they are, who believes they can be changed, and who works hard to make that change happen. We would not be sitting here celebrating a very great victory if it were not for such a person. Ladies and gentlemen, I give you Elaine Hadley, who found a way to change the world."

Then everybody stood up and drank a toast to me. Really. I didn't know where to look. Then Emma spilled her juice, and Roger tried to talk with his mouth full and spit chocolate cake onto Anastasia, and Petrie sneezed, and it was all right again.

"Hey! What about the great things *I* did?" Roger said.

Miss Applebaum smiled. "To Roger, who did great things." We ended up toasting everyone, which made me feel better.

I didn't think I'd be able to sleep after that, but I could hardly keep my eyes open.

Chapter 15

The greatest day of my life! INNOCENT TENANTS TRI-UMPH OVER NASTY LANDLORD. The Dutton Ceremony took place. It was a cold, cloudy November day, with a little snow falling, but I didn't care. We all stood on the porch. I handed Mr. Dutton the cheque we had worked so hard to get. It was hard to believe that I could hold so much money in my hand, on one slip of paper.

"What's this?" Dutton asked. His mouth fell open as he read it. "But this isn't possible!" he sputtered.

"Yes, it is!" I said, grinning.

Thornton stepped forward. "Edwin Archibald

Dutton, your contract with Mr. Wooley is now null and void. Kindly remove yourself from these premises. This is private property, owned by Mr. Wooley. And, oh yes. Here are your termination papers from the job as superintendent. Don't worry, all of this is strictly legal."

"But — "

"Don't try coming here again. All the locks have been changed, and your keys no longer fit."

"You couldn't have gotten so much money . . . My contract — "

"Hah! We did it, even if you don't like it!" Roger said.

"I don't understand."

"It isn't that complicated," Thornton said. "Mr. Wooley has discharged his debt to you by the deadline in your contract. You have no rights here anymore."

"You're history!" Roger shouted. "Get lost!"

"Yeah!" Emma said.

"In all my life," Dutton fumed, "I have never seen such a load of troublemakers!"

"Thank you!" Roger crowed.

"My lawyers will be going over these papers with a fine-toothed comb, and if there's anything even slightly underhanded about them — "

"Go over them all you like," Thornton said. "You won't find anything wrong. You have been beaten at your own game, Mr. Dutton. Go home!"

"Vamoose!" Roger cried. "Amscray!"

With a final glare at us, he left. We all cheered.
The Dutton War was over.

As Mr. Dutton drove away Thornton said. "I've never enjoyed myself so much! Do you have any other legal work you need help with, Elaine?"

"Who, me?" I said. Everyone laughed.

"Perhaps not at this time, dear boy," Miss Applebaum said.

"Are there any more of those triple-chocolate brownies left?" Thornton asked her.

"I took the precaution of making an extra batch this morning."

Mr. Wooley had enough money left over to put an especially fool-proof lock on the trapdoor, so now it can be used by workers to fix the roof (which is why it was built in the first place), but not used by anyone else, especially Emma. Mr. Trumpkin installed the lock for us. He hasn't called us hooligans for days.

Mom sent us to school late, with notes, after the Dutton Ceremony. When I got to class Petrie's articles about us were posted on the bulletin board and the whole class applauded. I felt funny, and I think my face turned red.

Mr. Wyman asked me to fill in the details. "I didn't know about any of this until I got around to reading Wednesday's newspaper," he said. "I don't get the Sunday paper. I wish you had told us what was going on, Laney. We would have loved to be part of your protest. People can't help you if they don't know you need help, you know."

"Yeah!" said some of the kids.

I had trouble talking in front of everyone at first. I still don't know a lot of them. But then it got easier. We spent the whole day talking about the way a newspaper works, and what the power of the press can and can't do.

"It's a lot harder being a reporter than I thought," I said.

"You can hand in your science project next week, with no penalty," Mr. Wyman told me at the end of the day. "And I think you should consider writing out this whole story."

"I already have," I said, "in my journal."

"I'll help you, if you'd like to bring it in."

After school I said to Roger, "You know, having an accident and hiding in your house for twenty years, and collecting over one hundred umbrellas seems kind of bizarre to me."

"You think so?" Roger said. His eyes shone. "Wow! I've got a bizarre story right here after all. I was right! I'll win the contest. I'll be rich and famous. People will send me their three-eyed frogs from all over the world!" His face took on a dreamy look. "Two-headed snails. Rats with wings. A house full of acrobatic slugs . . . "

"I hope not," I said. "Yuck!"

"Hey!" His eyes narrowed. "Why are you being nice to me?"

"Don't worry. It won't last. You're too much of a pain."

He grinned. "Thank you."

He's writing out his contest entry now while I finish up my journal.

LANEY'S LAW NUMBER 51:
It's great to be home.

Bev Spencer loves the idea of being able to learn and laugh at the same time. Maybe that's why she was once a clown, and why there's so much humour in *This Means War!* She has also been a songwriter and storyteller, and currently works as a librarian. (And given Laney's ambitions, it's possible that Bev would really have liked to be a World Famous Reporter!)

Bev's other books include *The Ghost of Sullivan Town*, *Paddy Martel Is Missing*, *Guardian of the Dark* and *Spaceship Down*. She is currently working on another novel about inner city kids.